LUD HE

IAIN SINCLAIR

LUD HEAT

a book of the dead hamlets~ May 1974 to April 1975

With an introduction by Allen Fisher and afterword by Michael Moorcock

Maps and illustrations by Brian Catling

This edition published in Great Britain in 2012 by Skylight Press, 210 Brooklyn Road, Cheltenham, Glos GL51 8EA

First published in Great Britain in 1975 by Albion Village Press, London.

Original illustrations and maps by Brian Catling
Cover photograph by Iain Sinclair
Designed and typeset by Rebsie Fairholm
Publisher: Daniel Staniforth
With thanks to Test Centre (www.testcentre.org.uk) for the map photo

Some of the poems, or earlier versions of them, have appeared in: *The Poetry Review*; *the Human Handkerchief* No. 5; *Great Works* 4; *The Curiously Strong* (Final Issue).

www.skylightpress.co.uk

Printed and bound in Great Britain by Lightning Source, Milton Keynes

British Library Cataloguing-in-Publication data:
A catalogue record for this book is available from the British Library.

ISBN 978-1-908011-60-2

To Iain Sinclair, on the publication of his book "LUD HEAT" in 1975

The more people communicate, by building-environments' symbolic natures as well as verbally, about their surroundings and social practice, the more they get to know about their place, enabling them to comprehend, thus appropriately deal with, their situations. It becomes increasingly necessary, in a society fashioned into obliged mobility, the jet set and tile economically insecure, to insist that home be made. That we "feel at home" whether as settlers and locals, or as nomads looking for rest in comfortable surroundings. At the same time it becomes necessary not to be fooled by, what at best is, the romanticism, the Ivor Novello, and, what at worst can lead to that blut-und-Boden Homeland propagated by the Third Reich. The necessity to locate, to place ourselves becomes increasingly apparent to people living, as you do Iain, in the throws (sic) of, up against the old walls of a city, when this City – London – is now one borough of 33 held in the name of The Greater Council. The idea of 'City', to someone in this situation, becomes of city dissolved, of an amoebic and pulsing cloak moving all bounds of geographic possibility leaving behind most bounds of etymological meaning in the name of City. To give sense of emotional attachment to locality, to the knowable and unrepeatable, does not mean to do so as an individual. The territorial ties are not made alone. There are subtle mechanisms at work subjugating our psyches, trying to keep and often succeeding to keep, our senses, awarenesses at a lower level than they need be in view of the social and economical potential of our situation. Kant held that enlightenment meant the liberation of people from the bondage for which they were themselves to blame. This is not to suggest that all you are concerned with is a matter of this rooting, but your symbolic concerns strongly relate to and impinge upon this area. Your work just is not semiotics. But *Lud Heat* assumes the kind of symbolic value particular architectural forms possess: what associations they are capable of evoking in individuals: what those associations depend on. Symbolic attachment to place, apart from the social relationships of groups, concerns itself primarily in the built urban environment. It is from these buildings that the energies of the area are – I was going to say, "generated".

The buildings you have "connected" have a common factor, and have common factor groups, without necessitating common "influence levels". They are, in your terms, generators. It is, you maintain, on these lines, or because of these lines of energy, that certain situations occur. Murder. Ritual Murder. Elevation. It remains outside of your concern to give measurable determinations of these forces. It might, however, be pertinent to note that the presence of William Blake's house in Hercules Road, Lambeth – or at least its site where many of Blake's books were etched – presents a psychical as well as physical presence for you. Blake's work presence is felt throughout the work, *Lud Heat*.

Your symbolic attachment of place is not merely that place given meaning by inherent attraction, by "magic", or by unaccountable attachment to soil. Nor is it solely the pyramidic structure of any of your "key" buildings. Needless to say it is not the buildings' functions to give this attachment. Your concern is energetic and about energy where the place becomes symbol of ourselves, or yourself, expressing that belonging by way of action. It is in inter-relationships of situational fields, lapping, overlapping. Where area, the town, becomes radius for action and where action takes place. Throughout *Lud Heat* evidence of this action is given. Evidences of intersections where the energies, on the map, in your consciousness and on the land come together and depart forming triangulations as those shown in Gordon's *Prehistoric London: Its Mounds and Circles*. But your connectors are more numerous and they include some of the people involved: your fellow garden workers; your wife and child are warmly dealt with adding an accuracy to the "placing" in the work. It is your perceiving, all-perceiving physically and psychically, that takes priority over the naming. Your namings focus the attention, but not the hands that mould, that sever. Your place is a pivot for memory weave between people: Sir Thomas Browne, Thomas De Quincey, Daniel Defoe, John Milton, &c.

Lud Heat has your "guided hand" but it is not the hand of "doctors, quacks, barbers, slaughtermen". Your hand holds the knife that cuts space and time, as Yeats' gyres do, as Hawksmoor's surveying made the "nome-wounds". Your *Lud Heat* works because you stake your claims, start from the situation you are in. Your landmarks are your short-hand symbols for city, Hawksmoor's churches your totems. Your territory is your possession purchased by your care and your work. The totems become yours and possess you and the work drawing on the energy, drawn by the energies of this London, produce the heat, the LUD HEAT.

Allen Fisher
from *Place* (Reality Street, 2005)

This book is for Joe, Arthur, Bill & the others who are in there for the duration.

This done, and after these things had been somewhat digested by Christiana and her company, the Interpreter takes them apart again, and has them first into a room where was a man that could look no way but downwards, with a muck-rake in his hand. There stood also one over his head, with a celestial crown in his hand, and proffered him that crown for his muck-rake; but the man did neither look up, nor regard, but raked to himself the straws, the small sticks, and dust of the floor.

Then said Christiana, I persuade myself that I know somewhat the meaning of this; for this is a figure of a man of this world; is it not, good Sir?

INTER. Thou has said the right, said he, and his muck-rake doth show his carnal mind. And whereas thou seest him rather give heed to rake up straws and sticks, and the dust of the floor, than to what he says that calls to him from above with the celestial crown in his hand, it is to show that heaven is but as a fable to some, and that things here are counted the only things substantial. Now, whereas it was also showed thee, that the man could look no way but downwards, it is to let thee know that earthly things, when they are with power upon men's minds, quite carry their hearts away from God.

CHRIS. Then said Christiana, Oh, deliver me from this muck-rake.

John Bunyan,
The Pilgrim's Progress

BOOK ONE
THE MUCK RAKE

NICHOLAS HAWKSMOOR, HIS CHURCHES

"All perils, specially malignant, are recurrent"
Thomas De Quincey (On Murder Considered As One Of The Fine Arts)

"The living can assist the imagination of the dead"
W. B. Yeats (A Vision)

The old maps present a sky-line dominated by church towers; those horizons were differently punctured, so that the subservience of the grounded eye, & the division of the city by nome-wound, was not disguised. Moving now on an eastern arc the churches of Nicholas Hawksmoor soon invade the consciousness, the charting instinct. Eight churches give us the enclosure, the shape of the fear; – built for early century optimism, erected over a fen of undisclosed horrors, white stones laid upon the mud & dust. In this air certain hungers were activated that have yet to be pacified; no turning back, as Yeats claims: "the stones once set up traffic with the enemy."

The Act of Parliament of 1711 provided taxes for the acquisition of sites, burial grounds, & parsonages. There was the rounded notion of 50 churches – but when the Commission for the Building of the New Churches discharged the Surveyors, Hawksmoor & John James, in 1733, only a dozen had been completed. Six, [St Alfege's, Greenwich/St Anne's, Limehouse/St George's-in-the-East/Christ Church, Spitalfields/St George's, Bloomsbury/St Mary Woolnoth], were wholly Hawksmoor's; he was also responsible for the obelisks at St Luke's, Old Street, & St John's, Horsleydown. He was the force behind the operation, the planning was in his hands. So that what we are talking about is not accident.

Hawksmoor, the Surveyor, examined & selected the sites, walked over the ground, drew up the plans, made wooden models, rapidly turned out a sequence of sketches, possible structures to contain some portion of his amazing polyglot energies. He had that frenzy, the Coleridge notebook speed, to rewrite the city – man recognising some distillation of his most private urges in the historical present, is suddenly, & more than anybody around him, *there* – had more to say than the 8 churches could use. So there are sketches cancelling sketches – & the churches themselves are incredible culture grafts, risky quotations studded into a central & repeated image of strength, key symbols that remain secret. The Commission required "one general design or forme". Hawksmoor worked to this, worked between the poles of Wren & Vanbrugh. Wren, practical, and Vanbrugh, extravagant, demanding that "a Temple ... should ever have the most Solemn & Awfull Appearance both without & within." Vanbrugh & the Commission condemned the practice of burial near the church – this, Hawksmoor ignored. He had his vision of the whole & he described it in a letter to Dr. George Clarke:

"we have noe City, nor Streets, nor Houses, but a Chaos of Dirty Rotten Sheds, allways tumbling or taking fire, with winding Crooked passages (scarse practicable) Lakes of Mud and Rills of Stinking Mire Running through them ... They had so favourable an opportunity to Rebuild London ye most August Towne in ye world, and either have Keept it to its old Dimention, or if it was reasonable to let it swell to a Larger, they ought for ye Publick good to have Guided it into a Regular and commodious form, and not have sufferd it to Run into an ugly inconvenient self destroying unweildly Monster."

The geometry of opposition was staked out, the work begun. We must examine the detail.

A triangle is formed between Christ Church, St George's-in-the-East & St Anne's, Limehouse. These are centres of power for those territories; sentinel, sphinx-form, slack dynamos abandoned as the culture they supported goes into retreat. The power remains latent, the frustration mounts on a current of animal magnetism, & victims are still claimed.

St George's, Bloomsbury, and St Alfege's, Greenwich, make up the major pentacle-star. The five card is reversed, beggars in snow pass under the lit church window; the judgement is "disorder, chaos, ruin, discord, profligacy." These churches guard or mark, rest-upon, two major sources of occult power: The British Museum & Greenwich Observatory – the locked cellar of words, the labyrinth of all recorded knowledge, the repository of stolen fires & symbols, excavated god-forms – & measurement, star-knowledge, time calculations, Maze Hill, the bank of light that faces the Isle of Dogs. So many spectres operate along these fringes: Yeats in the British Museum, at the time of the Ripper murders, researching into Blake – Blake & Newton, polar opposites. Milton; his early-morning walks over the ground where St George's was to be built. The only Hawksmoor church that could not be properly orientated.

Then there is the sub-system of fire obelisks: St Luke's, Old Street, & St John's, Horsleydown. They form an equilateral triangle, raised over the water, with London's true obelisk – "Cleopatra's Needle," which is, of course, the obelisk set up by Thothmes III in front of the Temple of the Sun at Heliopolis.

St Luke's obelisk (the church itself is decayed, the roof gone) stands over Bunhill Fields, plague pit, burial place of William Blake, Daniel Defoe, John Bunyan. Plague-year excavations discovering the antiquity of this site as a field of inhumation: pre-Roman. Defoe writes of it: "I have heard that in a great pit in Finsbury ... many who were infected & near their end, & delirious also, ran wrapped in blankets or rags & threw themselves in & expired there, before any earth could be thrown upon them." Milton died here, in his house at 125 Bunhill Row, "with so little pain or emotion, that the tide of his expiring was not perceived by those in the room." A sequence of heated incisions through the membranous time-layer.

Standing there, on a walk along the whole chain of Hawksmoor churches, we notice five minor obelisks in the fenced area beyond Blake's burial slab. The Old Street obelisk is aligned beyond the boundary wall: the point of force is discovered. We also come across a lichen diagram, the quadrivium, recognised later in that walk, the conflux of 4 roads beyond St George's-in-the-East, the place where the staked corpse of the Ratcliffe Highway killer was buried. This would relate to the labyrinth plans of the heart-shrine, the innermost sanctuary, scratched on the rock face outside the Palaeolithic Cave.

St John's, Horsleydown, lies to the south of Tower Bridge, in the bent elbow of Druid Street, across the water from Tower Hill, burial place of the immortal head of Bran. It is destroyed, a rim of old bricks upon which an office-block has been erected. The obelisk is gone, though we can still walk directly out of Druid Street into Crucifix Lane and down St Thomas Street to the preserved surgical tower, known to John Keats & Sir William Gull.

We can mark out the total plan of the churches on the map & sift the meanings. We can produce the symbol of Set, instrument of castration or tool for making cuneiform signs. To maim or to mark. The shaman is eunuch.

The scenographic view is too complex to unravel here, the information too dense; we can only touch on a fraction of the possible relations. The Tower is obviously central, a fixed point. The lesser vertebrae support the wings of the beast. The web is printed on the city & disguised with multiple superimpositions. We can still follow one direct line of escape: Christ Church – Bunhill Fields – St Luke's – the Penton Mound & Suicide Ponds – Parliament Hill. The returning arrow is equally interesting: St George's, Bloomsbury – Cleopatra's Needle – Blake's Lambeth. And the connecting rod, the straight line from Hercules Road to Christ Church passes, of course, through St Mary Woolnoth, Hawksmoor's pulpit of slave sermons, attacks on the blood trade. Christ Church is in alignment with St George's in-the-East & St Alfege's. St George's-in-the-East & St Luke's are equidistant from Christ Church, etc., – This is another whole work. It is enough to sketch the possibilities.

From what is known of Hawksmoor it is possible to imagine that he did work a code into the buildings, knowingly or unknowingly, templates of meaning, bands of continuing ritual. The building should be a Temple, an active place, a high metaphor. The buildings taken together, knotted across the city, yield a further word. Hawksmoor's obituary tells us that "he was a very skilful Mathematician, Geographer & Geometrician ... perfectly skill'd in the History of Architecture, & could give an exact Account of all the famous Buildings, both Ancient & Modern, in every part of the World." He worked, quietly, to a position of public influence: Deputy Surveyor at Winchester, with Wren at Greenwich, college commissions at Oxford, the mausoleum park & pyramid complex at Castle Howard. Died of "gout in the stomach." His motives remain opaque; his churches are the mediums, filled with the dust of wooden voices.

The plans for the unrealised "Basilica After The Primitive Christians" give us a glimpse at the ambition of Hawksmoor's London operation. This was his ideal or archetype. It was to be laid out to the east of Brick Lane, alongside Hare Marsh, where the Kray brothers' pub, the Carpenter's Arms, now stands. He wanted a "Septum or Enclosure ... to keep off filth Nastyness & Brutes." This hope is also unrealised.

The churches are only one system of energies, or unit of connection, within the city – the old hospitals, the Inns of Court, the markets, the prisons, the religious houses are the others. They have their disciples, aware of the older relations.

Each church is an enclosure of force, a trap, a sight-block, a raised place with an unacknowledged influence on events enacted within their nome-lines.

Certain features are in common: extravagant design, massive, almost slave-built, strength – not democratic. A strength that is not connected to notions of "craftsmanship" or "elegance". They are not easy on the eye, & do not enforce images of grace. Metaphors inflate at their own risk. The mind is not led upwards

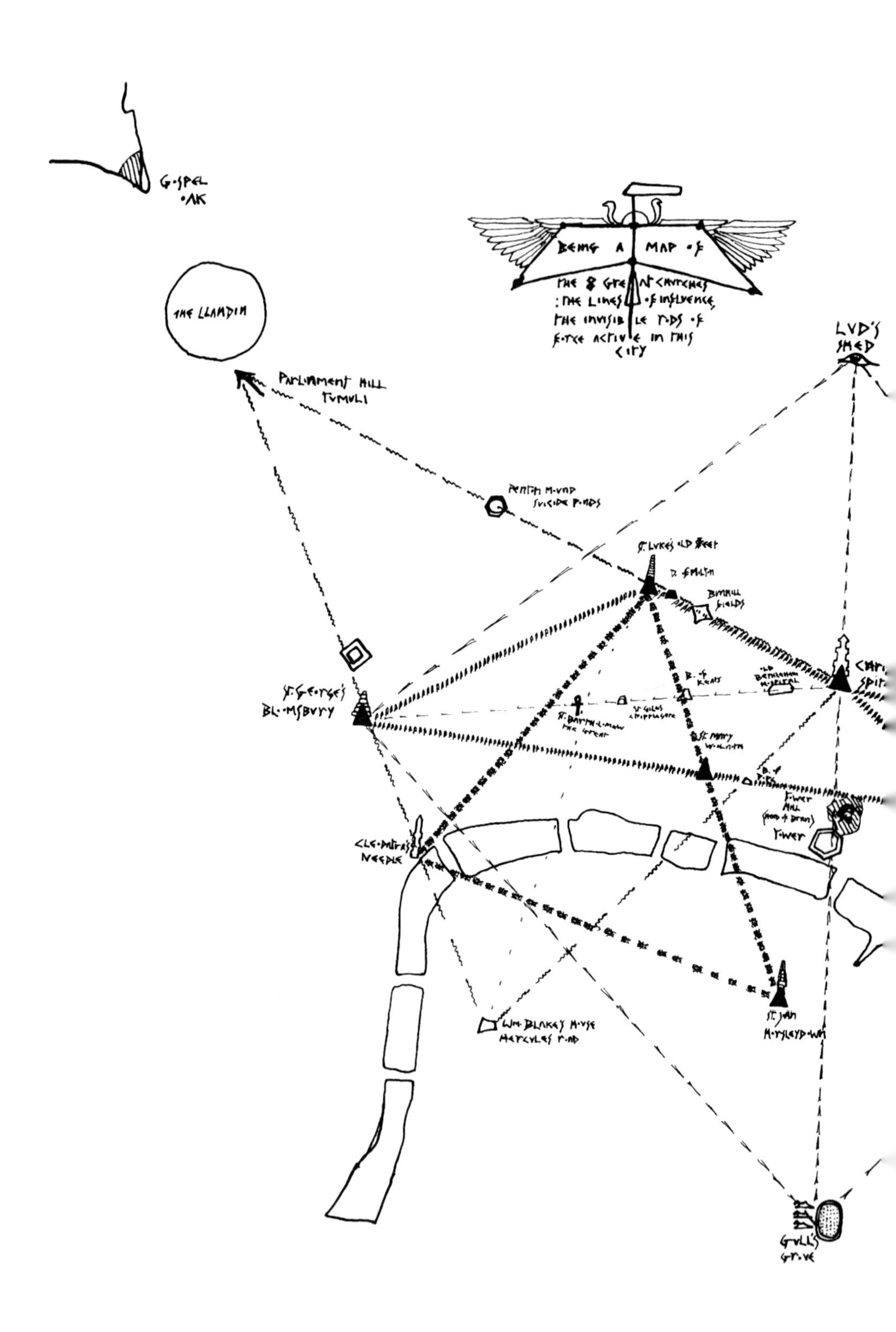
Gospel Oak
The Llandin
Being a map of the 8 great churches: the lines of influence, the invisible rods of force active in this city
Lud's Shed
Parliament Hill Tumuli
Penton Mound Suicide Ponds
St. Luke's Old Street
B. of Milton
Bunhill Fields
B. of Keats
Old Bethlehem Hospital
Chri
Spit
St. George's Bloomsbury
St. Bartholomew the Great
St Giles Cripplegate
St. Mary Woolnoth
B. of Pepys
Tower Hill (Hung & Drawn)
Tower
Cleopatra's Needle
Wm. Blake's House Hercules Road
St. John Horsleydown
Gull's Grove

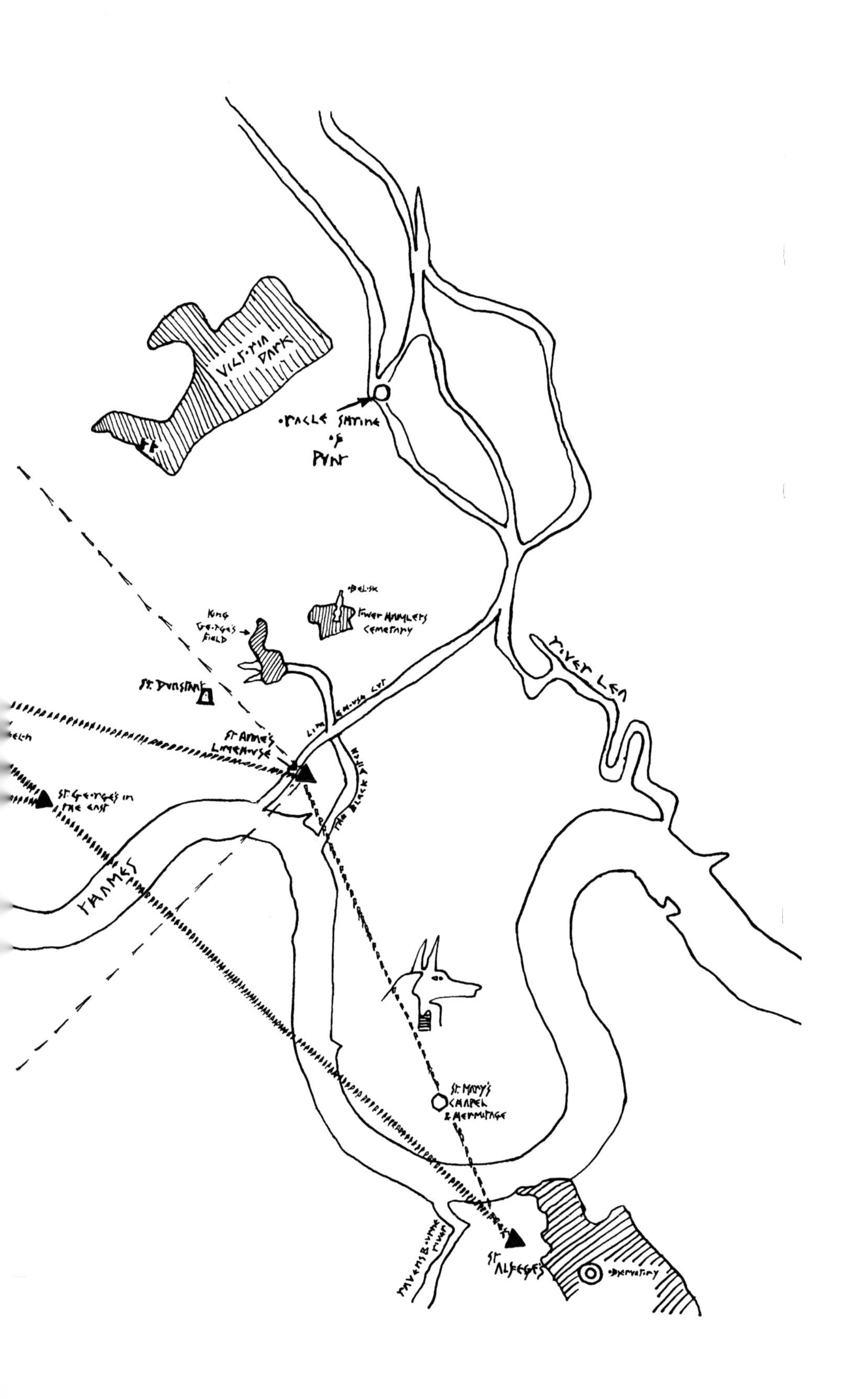

Victoria Park
Oracle Shrine of Pan
Obelisk
Tower Hamlets Cemetary
King George's Field
St. Dunstan's
St Anne's Limehouse
Limehouse Cut
The Black Ditch
River Lea
St George's in the East
Thames
St Mary's Chapel & Hermitage
Ravensbourne River
St Alfege's
Observatory

to any starry nest. These buildings do not hide & yet are not much in the consciousness or conversations of present parishioners – it is there, but you have to dig for it. There is no Chartres or Salisbury feel, with the church as the excuse for everything else. It shocks every time you glimpse one of the towers. They are shunned. Their strength is hybrid, awkward: an admix of Egyptian & Greek source matter – curiosities discovered in engraved library plates. Necropolis Culture. Behemoths from the Zoo of Abortions. Botched Sphinx experiments. The Great Mausoleum at Halicarnassus is re-enacted in Bloomsbury. You can see it in the background of Hogarth's "Gin Lane". And this is appropriate. The east London churches still draw the meths-men & derelicts, fire-alcohol devotees, to the attendant parks. The mendicants have escaped from the Five of Pentacles. They rest on gravestones & benches. This is almost medieval. They are waiting, hanging around, debating; ferocious solitary monologues – in the clutch of root instincts. It is the opening shot of a lepers' pilgrimage. Hard charity is expected. Scourges & soup-kitchens. Sanctuary. The church not altogether benevolent, but seducing these terminal optimists into some tall parental grasp. British White Wine bottles smash against the numbered steps: the broken fragments of brown glass are part of the design. The walls are varnished with urine. They study & inscribe the graffiti with prophetic seriousness.

There is a further possible reading to the vagrant invasion of these vestry-protected lands – that they have come to consult the oracle that can no longer be discovered – made their cross-country journeys by well-worn migration tracks to extinguish ego in the bladed flame – that they have been prematurely released, by catastrophe & shock, from the incubation cubicles beneath the church – half resolved dream victims – half-cured – they babble of the vision which they carry as identity.

My own jobs follow the churches across the city. Cigar-packing in Clerkenwell & I cycle past St Luke's, the obelisk to my right, Bunhill Fields to my left. Ullage cellars of Truman's Brewery, Brick Lane, & I front Christ Church. Garden assistant, & grass manicurist, in Limehouse & I mow continually between the shifting influence of St George's & St Anne's.

I spoke of the unacknowledged magnetism & control-power, built-in code force, of these places; I would now specify ... the ritual slaying of Marie Jeanette Kelly in the ground floor room of Miller's Court, Dorset Street, directly opposite Christ Church ... the Ratcliffe Highway slaughter of 1811, with the supposed-murderer, stake through heart, trampled into the pit where four roads cross to the north of St George's-in-the-East ... the battering to death of Mr Abraham Cohen, summer 1974, on Cannon Street Road, one spoke of the quadrivium: £110,000 in old bank-notes in the kiosk behind him, stuffed in cocoa tins & cigarette packets; three ritualistic coins laid at his feet, as they were in 1888 at the feet of Mary Ann Nicholls, the first Ripper victim.

Each of these events deserves more detailed consideration than fits with this brief & nervy synopsis. The whole karmic programme of Whitechapel in 1888 moves around the fixed point of Christ Church, that Tower of the Winds – from the east in – closer & closer, until the risk of the final act is achieved, purgation/completion – performed in the decay of a pseudo-crypt.

We cannot leave Christ Church without mentioning the curious detail of the windows (which is echoed in the street-facing wall of Truman's Brewery, Brick Lane) – the pull that is set up by the sequence of small circular portholes above tall narrow lower windows. This is the symbol at the heart of Munch's iconography – & relates to a whole chain of meanings & resonances – the grail-cup above the lance – the cauldron & the sword – female & male – the setting sun & the molten light over the waters – the pill about to be dropped into the test-tube – stylization of the phallus & generative spurt – volatile/active – demanding the leap of energies – repeated symbols of the unconsummated – invitation. Kerry Downes thinks of the portholes as tunnels into the masonry, locking us deeper into the shape of the building.

Hawksmoor discovered a translatable version of this in the 12th century English towers at Exeter, Norwich & Ely.

If Christ Church was magnet to the archetypal murder myth of the late nineteenth century, St George's-in-the-East was host to the definitive fear-prose of the early century: "a work more lasting than brass ... the most superb of the century by many degrees ... the sublimest & most entire in their excellence that ever were committed" as De Quincey claimed in his celebrated postscript to *Murder Considered as One of the Fine Arts*. The Ratcliffe Highway murders.

De Quincey in his best Paramount purple sketches the "local scene" ... "Ratcliffe Highway is a public thoroughfare in a most chaotic quarter of eastern or nautical London ... manifold ruffianism shrouded impenetrably under the mixed hats & turbans of men whose past was untraceable to any European eye ... Lascars, Chinese, Moors, Negroes ..."; but there is no mention of the church motor, even though much of the responsibility in seeking out the criminal lay with St George's Vestry. The essay, a brilliant narrative of high journalism & spine-tickling, was obviously assembled at a distance, by purely psychic connection. It did not grow from direct observation of the ground – so that the major visual clue was missed.

The affair is treated as a straight-forward scenario of brute force, pre-Dostoyevsky; the in-cold-blood entry of domestic enclosures & the massacre of all innocents found within. Two groups destroyed, the Marrs & the Williamsons. The Marrs living on ground that Hawksmoor had attempted to persuade the Commission to buy, so that he could extend St George's frontage. But De Quincey, at his speed & exhaustion of operation, fending off the monkey, digressing obsessively towards overlapping versions of the truth, couldn't help getting in among the authentic sub-strata. Unconsciously he offers hieroglyphs, disguised & smudged Egyptian ritual detail. "To one invariable type all the murders ... conformed: the skull was first shattered; this step secured the murderer from

instant retaliation; and, then, by way of locking up all into eternal silence, uniformly the throat was cut." No rationale for this second act. The precise observance that was favoured in Whitechapel. The windpipe severed, the throat cut with the same left-handed stroke. The butchery was formal. Hieratic imposing on demotic. The guided hand. Suspicion of all doctors, quacks, barbers, slaughtermen.

This is made even clearer in De Quincey's description of the death of the Marr baby. There was, of course, no logical reason for killing a creature who could make no coherent witness; but the murderer seems to have been pushed into a wheel of frenzy, forced towards pre-sculptural image making.

"... The next ominous sign was, that the hood of the cradle had been smashed to pieces. It became evident that the wretch had found himself doubly embarrassed — first, by the arched hood, at the head of the cradle which accordingly he had beat into a ruin with his mallet, and secondly, by the gathering of the blankets & pillows about the baby's head. The free play of his blows had thus been baffled. And he had therefore finished the scene by applying his razor to the throat of the little innocent; after which, with no apparent purpose, as though he had become confused by the spectacle of his own atrocities, he had busied himself in piling the clothes elaborately over the child's corpse."

Then there are the clues in word selection, similes, chosen at speed, against time, the random adjectives ... "most insinuating & snaky refinement" ... "has energy enough to jump up again, like a pyramid of fire, & soar high above ruin many times repeated" ... "a dexterous movement of his left hand" ... "to notice the absolute certainty with which the silent hieroglyphics of the case betray to us the whole process & movements of the bloody drama."

Finally there is the murderer's hair:

"... the most extraordinary & vivid colour, viz., bright yellow, something between an orange & a lemon colour. Williams had been in India; chiefly in Bengal & Madras; but he had also been upon the Indus. Now, it is notorious that, in the Punjab, horses of a high caste are often painted — crimson, blue, green, purple;

& it struck me that Williams might, for some casual purpose of disguise, have taken a hint from this practice of Scande & Lahore ..."

The hint may have been taken, but not for any "casual purpose of disguise." It is the imprecise itch of ritual observance coming through again.

It was a time of confusion & chaos, as in 1888, tangled motives, half-delivered impulses. Nobody, guilty or innocent, seems to have quite known what they were doing. The transcripts of the witnesses are full of cancelled stories, lies, wrong dates, infinitely adjustable times. The possible assassins were many – a whole cross-section of villains were activated – & it is impossible to say who actually struck the blows & who were ready to do it. The pattern of arrest, statement, release, allowed many obscure fringe figures to escape the net. There was, for example, Cahill (Ka-Hill) who was found and brought back from Marlborough, where he had, for no reason that he could articulate, wandered to the edges of Avebury & Silbury Hill.

The mass hostility to the corpse of Williams was of a unified beast ferocity. The entire population of the district rose with the aim of destroying him, dismembering him & working every savagery upon his dead flesh. But the violence was formalised, a ritual was invented. A solemn procession from St George's where the body had been kept overnight, a loop was made

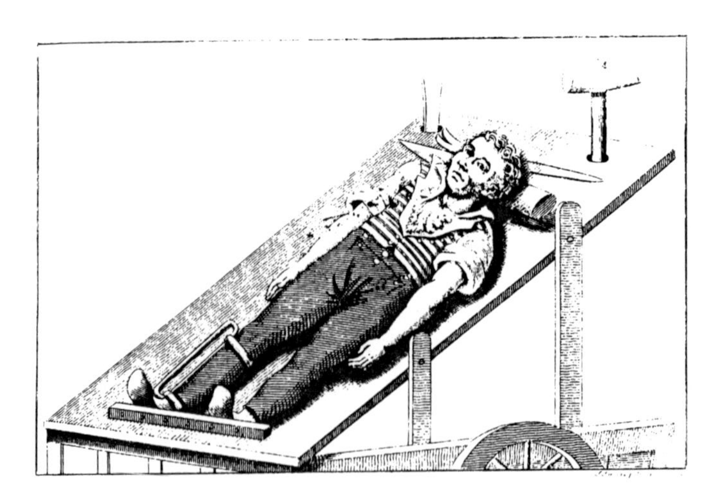

through the district, that all might see – past the Pear Tree where Williams had lodged – the Williamsons' pub – the Marrs' Ratcliffe Highway shop – St George's – to the place of burial. The cart that carried the body had been specially prepared with murder weapons, maul & chisel, exhibited, as well as the stake. De Quincey does not talk much about this, mentioning only that after Williams hanged himself ... "he was buried in the centre of a quadrivium, or conflux of four roads (in this case four streets), with a stake driven through his heart. And over him drives for ever the uproar of unresting London."

The year was 1812, the church very nearly one hundred years old, Blake writing *Jerusalem* ...

"And every Act a Crime, and Albion the punisher & judge ...
... He hath compell'd Albion to become a Punisher ...
... London is a stone of her ruins ...
... the murder'd bodies of her little ones ...
... What shall I do? what could I do if I could find these Criminals?
I could not dare to take vengeance ...
... So spake Los, travelling thro' darkness & horrid solitude;
And he beheld Jerusalem ...
... Among the ruins of the Temple, and Vala who is her Shadow,
Jerusalem's Shadow, bent northward over the Island white.
At length he sat on London Stone & heard Jerusalem's voice."

And more, the procession, the chain of body images & solar fires, punishments, ecstasies, planetary revenge: ENERGY.

Swedenborg, the feeder & source for Blake, was buried in Wellclose Square, alongside the Ratcliffe Highway, the immediate neighbour of St George's. It is even conceivable, according to Kerry Downes, that Hawksmoor helped Cibber to design the Danish Church. "O Swedenborg! strongest of men, the Samson shorn by the Churches, shewing the Transgressors in Hell, the proud Warriors in Heaven, Heaven as a Punisher, & Hell as One under Punishment." The body has now been dug up & shipped back to Sweden but the name remains in the ground: Swedenborg Gardens.

The Marrs lie on the south-side of the churchyard of St George's, but Williams' mutilated & broken corpse has been taken out from under Cannon Street Road, his bones scattered. The skull was stolen – possession of the talisman passes from publican to publican – it was for a time at the Crown & Dolphin – but is now lost in rumour.

These facts fade. The big traffics slam by. A work ethic buries ancient descriptions.

February 4, 1974, & I endure an apocalyptic dream of the moon disk growing, crashing down on the city, burying itself in the tower of St Anne's, Limehouse. It is the Tarot of the Moon: "hidden enemies, danger, calumny, darkness, terror, deception, occult forces, error." I had not then seen the church by daylight, but recognised it immediately on my first day as a gardener.

There had been one prior visit, by night. We had gone to Regent's Canal Dock, beyond Stepney East, in pursuit of the rumour of water vegetation Dagon ghost presences at this place. We walked across from Hackney: Globe Road, White Horse Lane, St Dunstan's, a bricked-up terrace, LEB OFF, that ran towards Stepney East station – white light flashes on the low clouds, elevated electrical faults on the railway. Into the warren:

Juniper Street, Redcastle Place, Elf Row, Glamis Place, Butcher Row – & there is the black oil water & the punctured cauliflower, cloud helmet, around St Anne's. The church oversees the dock. And we are surprised to discover on a hump in the grounds a white stone pyramid.

The Hawksmoor churches have a close connection with burial sites, Roman & pre-Roman. The Romans regarded east London not as a place for the living but as a necropolis for the dead. The Mithraic Mysteries were confined within the city walls. Christ Church rises out of Spitalfields, which was excavated in 1574 when the brickfields, from which Brick Lane gets its name, were being dug. Bone masses were then discovered; cartloads. Ashes. Powder. Skulls. Stone coffins. It is interesting to see again the progress that is true of many of the present London Markets: burial ground/Hospice/market. Vegetable in this case. Smithfield takes the meat route: Templar Hospice/Tournament Field/Fair/Place of Martyrdom Fire/Hospital.

Ratcliffe, which lies to the south of St George's, is an even earlier burial ground: Red Cliff, – overlooking Wapping, the hanging dock, place of execution, the chained bodies washed over & fed by three tides. An ornate sarcophagus was removed from Ratcliffe Field during building work in the 17th century.

And I connect the present churches to this mood. Relate them to the four Egyptian protector-goddesses, guardians of the canopic jars. I associate the churches with rites of autopsy on a more than local scale.

St Alfege's, the first church, is represented by Isis 𓊨𓏏𓆇. Nephthys 𓉠 guards St George's-in-the-East. Neith 𓋋𓏏, the woman wearing the red crown, has to be present in Christ Church. Selkis 𓊃𓂋𓏏, the scorpion goddess associated with the scorching heat of the sun, must have St Anne's.

That was my hunch: confirmation followed. Sunstroke at Limehouse church; – & then the fact brought out at a lecture on "Roman London" by the Egyptologist, P. Clayton, that a fragment of a coarseware jug, dedicated to Isis, had been found on the foreshore of the Thames not far from St Anne's.

We are pushed towards the notion of these churches as Temples; & as cult-centres. Courts & gardens where the living communicate with the dead & receive wisdom from them. St Anne's seems to connect closely with the 'Mortuary House' which C. E. Joel writes of in "Megalith into Pyramid" (*New Diffusionist*, July '74):

"... the Valley Building ... was situated on the bank of the Nile where the funerary procession in its boat was disembarked for the final stage of the proceedings. In the fully developed pyramid complex this building was a small but elaborately designed structure of stone ... the design may have arisen from a hypothetical former pavilion of a less durable nature, a structure of matting on a framework of poles lashed together with ropes, which may have been the building called in ancient texts set-netjer *(pavilion-of-the-God). On one interpretation this structure served two purposes, as the 'Purification-tent' & as the 'House-of-Embalmment' ... Furthermore, it is also suggested that after this temporary mat pavilion had been translated into a stone building, the purification ceremony still took place in a mat pavilion erected on its stone roof."*

St Anne's fulfils many of these requirements: as geographical & spiritual site. We have the possibility of access by water for the funerary procession – the Church opening onto Limehouse Cut. St Anne's is, in fact, an island shrine; stands at the base of the great lingam of the Isle of Dogs, the Pool of Testes aimed at Greenwich Hill, St Alfege's.

"Thy heart is dilated with joy, the Pool of Testes becometh satisfied. Seth hath fallen, his two hands are hacked off, cuts asunder the knife his joints."

We find reason enough for the haunted dock, the light upon water, the climbing vegetation, the paths of observance. And the elaborate design, the fanciful arrangements of brick, take on meaning. The raised symbols are no longer random. The stone translation is not word perfect, its gematria is not made with full consciousness: accidents occur.

The forecourt of St Anne's, & of the other churches, is the area set aside for sacrifice & ceremonies of fire; first ritual of purification. Christ Church opens to the market & is surrounded by chicken slaughter houses, kosher & Bangladeshi cages & fly-curtained back rooms. The larger human sacrifices already mentioned must be taken as over-reaction, excess of zeal, or assigned to the full tide of late-century fears, the ninth gyre, messianic spasms found in Sioux Ghost dances, dervish vision, Golden Dawn sitting rooms.

The forecourt of St Anne's reaches back, through an early Christian sense of protected dwelling-place & stable, to the church as host. In the gardens that back onto this area may be found a goat & several collections of chickens. The tomb-keeper, Wag (Wepwawet?), is not above filling his garage with rabbits. His familiar is the dog, wolf-headed patroller of the pyramid. Wag, the legend-maker, also claims an underground passage between his crumbling house ("where Charles Dickens used to stay") & the crypt of the church; – which would fit with C. E. Joel's analogy of long-barrow chamber tombs & the Valley Building of the pyramid complex.

"It is in the forecourt area around the entrance to the passage which leads to the burial chamber that is found such evidence as survives of the rites carried out when a body was being interred. Of these, fires & animal sacrifices are the most definite. Signs of burning occur in various forms, patches of ashes, areas of scorched earth & stone & pieces of burnt bone."

The walls beside the steps & the crypt exterior stones are blackened by fire. The tomb carvings offer evidence of fire worship.

The steps of the church lend themselves to the mathematics of Osiris: the Nine. Climbing to this number yields the mystic position where vision is at its most powerful. Eye travels out through the hoop of the gate. On this step we achieve weightlessness & lift, momentarily, into an extended plane. Behind us is the enclosed staircase, the Wind Tower, the crypt entrance, the hidden spiral of steps, down to the incubation cubicles – "oracular dream cures took place in side chapels" (G. R. Levy).

Sir Thomas Browne is the laureate of this mood. As he says: "to subsist in bones & be but pyramidically extant is a fallacy in duration" ... or again ... "if Aegyptian Philosophy may obtain, the scale of influences was thus disposed, & the geniall Spirits of both worlds do trace their way in ascending & descending pyramids, mystically apprehended by the letter X." Pyramids, their meaning.

Hawksmoor was obsessed/possessed by pyramids – continually working them into his draft sketches – the cubical lanterns at the eastern corners of St Anne's, in the 1716 version, are crowned by tall pyramids – which the masons omitted. Masonic Time versus Pyramid Time. It could have torn the pins out of the whole structure, so that the beast would have shaken itself to dust. The idea of the Temple built above water, natural rock spring, travelling at one speed with the earth; placed, solid – opposed & countered by a defiant edge of preservation-time – the empty coffin – chamber moving too fast to be seen – shrinks in time – defeat of the despotic eye. Again / the pencil drawings of 1716-7 – "the stage above the belfry supports a sort of pyramid ending in a large Ionic capital, perhaps made of lead" (Kerry Downes): omitted by the masons. The constant drag of day-to-day reality / practical considerations blunts the overt statement of high ritual, the claim of kinship. So that the more obvious symbols, the elevated pyramids, are excluded – while the arcane & disguised, the subversive sentences get through, and are still operational.

St Anne's, in plan, is seen to be closely related to the horned scorpion gate form, as described by G. R. Levy; *The Tombs of the Giants*, Sardinia. And this goes back, once more, to Egypt – not by direct route, carried in migration; the plodding cultural transfer theory – but by sap connection – archetypal expression of common needs & badges – it is the essential shape of a particular kind of fear. Hathor the Mother Goddess, whose horns hold up the moon disk – so the February dream is apposite, pre-vision – & the church is the goddess is the body is the house – contains Osiris – by assimilation. Our rapid spirits trace out a moving

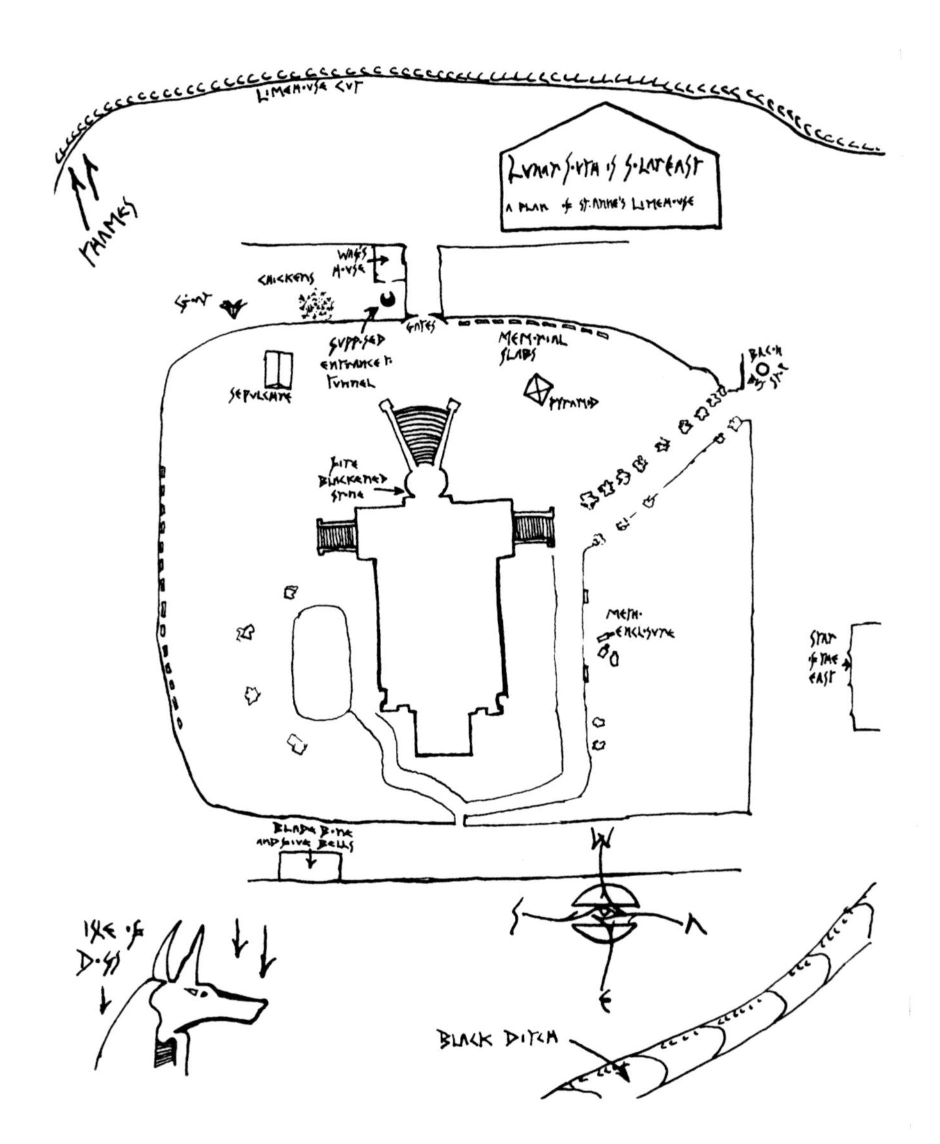
LIMEHOUSE CUT
THAMES
LUNAR SOUTH IS SOLAR EAST
A PLAN OF ST. ANNE'S LIMEHOUSE
WAG'S HOUSE
CHICKENS
SUPPOSED ENTRANCE TO TUNNEL
GATES
MEMORIAL SLABS
SEPULCHRE
PYRAMID
SITE BLACKENED STONE
MEMO. ENCLOSURE
STAR OF THE EAST
BLADE BONE AND SEVEN BELLS
ISLE OF DOGS
BLACK DITCH

cage of paths & tracks around the pyramid – are bees – pieces of the sun – under the sign of the winged eye – the influence of the great emblems – Lily, Bee, Vulture, Snake – serve the church. The conception is chthonic & underlies the construction of the temple. The temple is a map of the idea – built to accommodate the desire of the god – a sacrifice – that the god might enter the hollowed body, in fire, & be present – his word – the church is a mummified bee surrounded by water – the sycamore is here – the acknowledged body of Hathor – feeding the ground with milky fluids – the ground feeding the tree with the emanations of the gathered dead. The fruit of the union is Osiris, whose corpse is scattered, is divided up into the 8 churches. The tree is folded about him. He is in the movement of its branches. His words are loosed upon the city, are not regarded. And the river journey of Osiris is repeated, again & again, in the funerary processions of his worshippers, in the rising & falling of tides.

There is a token pyramid in the ground alongside each of the churches: to the south of Christ Church / to the east of St George's / to the west of St Anne's. These pyramids are the removed brains: the first & most essential of the autoptic acts. The brains being removed through the nose by puncturing the ethmoid bone. Held under white stone. They must be activated by the chanted word of need to animate the shell of the building, to bring life to the beast.

St Anne's is again the truest fulfilment of the Egyptian prototype. We are told (in the British Museum *Introductory Guide to the Egyptian Collections*) that:

"on the east side of the Great Pyramid is the mortuary temple, in which the funerary cult of the dead king was practised, & from it a stone causeway leads to the edge of the desert to the ... Valley temple in which the final rites were performed on the body of the king before it was taken to the pyramid."

So what has happened here is a reversal in scale: that the mortuary temple has been enlarged, its function swollen – & the pyramid, the astral power, been reduced. Natural & ancient rhythms are perverted in Golgonooza's architectures. Tho'

Hawksmoor, at least, had a sense of the paradigm, the condition of light, that had to be pursued.

At St Anne's the church (Mortuary Temple) is to the east of the pyramid ... the stone causeway (the Highway, becoming Commercial Road & West Ferry Road) does lead to the desert, the great swamp of the Isle of Dogs, which did hold a single chapel, now destroyed, its only ritual focus. Or, alternatively, we can read St George's as the Mortuary Temple (the body of Williams) with the Highway connecting to St Anne's on the edge of the desert, as the place of final rites.

These pyramids can claim a relation with the lost pyramids of Glastonbury that flanked the burial place of Arthur, that mythologist's bottomless pit. M. R. James writes of them:

"Among the strange old things at Glastonbury which I most regret ... were certain structures which William of Malmesbury calls 'pyramids' of stone, in the cemetery, carved with figures & inscriptions which even in his time were difficult to make anything of. They went back to the period of Celtic influence, & I cannot but suppose that they were something in the nature of the 'high crosses' of Ireland ... No fragment has ever turned up which can be supposed to have belonged to one of these ..."

Herodotus was also interested in these structures, himself an initiate:

"Wishing to go one better than his predecessors on the throne Asychis built a pyramid of brick to commemorate his reign, & on it cut an inscription in stone to the following effect: do not compare me to my disadvantage with the stone pyramids. I surpass them as far as Zeus the other gods. They pushed a pole to the bottom of a lake, & the mud which stuck on it they collected and made into bricks. That was how they built me."

The location of this pyramid fits in the present context:

"The site of the building is almost an island, for two canals have been led from the Nile & sweep round it, one on each side, as far as the entrance ..."

Which is St Anne's: whose arms are the Limehouse Cut & the River Lea. She stands at the gate of the swamp, the Isle of Dogs; Anubis guarded, Jackal, patron of embalmers, chief citizen of the Necropolis. A tainted place, as Pepys records:

"So we were fain to stay there, in the unlucky Isle of Dogs, in a chill place, the night cold, to our great discomfort."

It is not mere supposition that Hawksmoor & Herodotus were linked. We find a scribble on Hawksmoor's Mausoleum plans for Castle Howard, a sketch for "The Belvidera / After Ye Antique vid. Herodotus / Pliny & M: Varo".

The churches live in accordance with so many sacred conditions. They are sited by water & by springs: – we know now that an underground stream passes beneath the Christ Church foundations – that St Anne's, St George's, & St Alfege's all front the Thames – that Anne's border is Limehouse Cut – as Alfege's is the Ravensbourne River, becoming Deptford Creek. Water, the sex element, dark purifications, change, maternal suicide invitation; responding, dominating – allowing the buildings a connection, making them part of one body. "MY NECK IS OF ISIS THE DIVINE. MY FOREARMS ARE OF NEITH, LADY OF SAIS."

And if there is the generous (female) birth of light there is also the red claw of vengeance: Christ Church & St George's-in-the-East. George is Sphinx, a lion body sprawling along the Highway – "terrible, living" – as are the four lions of the south-gate of Golgonooza. "LUNAR SOUTH IS SOLAR EAST" (Yeats). St George's is Blake's East in *The Marriage of Heaven & Hell:* "spiritual wrath." The lions of Urizen forge the geometric shapes that underlie the material universe.

"Then siez'd the Lions of Urizen their work, & heated in the forge
Roar the bright masses; thund'ring beat the hammers, many a (Globe del.) *pyramid*
Is form'd & thrown down thund'ring into the deeps of Non Entity.

. . .

For measur'd out in order'd spaces, the Sons of Urizen
With compasses divide the deep; they the strong scales erect
That Luvah rent from the faint Heart of the Fallen Man,
And weigh the massy (Globes del.*) Cubes, then fix them in their awful stations."*

Urizen named his 30 African cities: Egypt. "Pharaoh in his iron Courts & the Dragon of the River & the Furnaces of Iron." River / Dragon ... St George's again. Dagon. Nephthys, the canopic guardian assigned to this church, was supposedly a female Neptune, threatening inundation, that the River must flood its banks & make the dry soil fertile. These mistranslations give us the swamp-lands of Wapping & the Isle of Dogs. Or Blake engraving Fuseli's *Fertilization of Egypt*. The description in Foster Damon's Dictionary:

" ... he interpreted an Egyptian god as the blind cry of the flesh, the prayer of the animal which is in us all. The dog-headed Anubis faces inward; his uplifted hands pierce the cloud-barrier as he appeals to Sirius, the dim, six-pointed Dog Star. But all stars are Urizen's, and it is Urizen who answers the prayer with lightnings & storm-floods of water. Blake added a musical instrument, a systrum, lying neglected on a bank; hinting that a means of invoking true deity was being overlooked."

And this is the other coding at St George's, the curvature & stony design of an unplayed musical score. Spiral form notation. Church as instrument. Unregistered pitch.

The speed of the track increases & information fattens to excess. It is the greasy slope of madness, time-bends, over stimulated blood hooks at the high air. Blake is too bright to be looked into – even at this distance. The whole structure becomes top-heavy & falls beyond control. Mark out a possible ground-plan for further & more calmly detailed studies. Speak of the excitement that is still there. Acknowledge energy.

The sun culture is a danger – too hot for random flirtations – to hold up that sign in the crow town, Llyn Din; to affront the buried head of Bran. Hawksmoor, bird name, climbs above Wren's civilizing city patterns. Fires his wing: – Herodotus tells

us that "the obelisk is the symbol of the Sun God at Heliopolis" – Lautreamont warns that "the weight of an obelisk stifles the spread of madness" – Hawksmoor risks an obelisk over the grave of William Blake. He understood its meaning, the clenched stomach cancer fears, and managed to pen his *Explanation of the Obelisk* (Blenheim Library):

"an obelisk. On the Apex (or Top) of the Shaft, may be placed a Star ... The French Set up an Obelisk at Arles ... On the Top was placed the Sun ... But that (parhelion) or false Sun, was forced, to Leave Shineing by the Influence of a British Star, the brightest Europe has yet at any time, ever Seen ..."

What cosmic order does he affront, or do we affront by raking over these old wound paths in this Year of the Tiger? Breaking the code of the churches gives us twin fears: fire & inundation. These holy places are ashlar-faced tombs of the sacred crocodile ... or they demand sacrificial flame. Consume, consummate: God's place. Possession of the hollow body by demonic, multi-tongued, fires.

St Anne's was gutted by fire on the morning of Good Friday, April 6, 1850. Vernal Equinox, time of occult threat. The organ pipes were melted by the heat – the altar windows & all wall-monuments were destroyed. Ceremonies continued to be performed – in the Vestry, above the crypt stairs. Can we connect into the same grid of influence the incendiary insects that fell on London in the 1939-45 war – the nights of firestorm zoned into these targets? In the blitz of 1941 St George's was gutted by fire-bombs – It remains a mummified shell. And, interestingly, Cleopatra's Needle was scarred during the first ever raid on London by a German Aeroplane, a few minutes before midnight, 1917.

The second fear is also confirmed in the texts: flood. Maitland's *History of London:*

"The Chapel House in the Isle of Dogs, or Poplar Marsh; is the Ruins of a Stone Chapel, but when, or by whom built is unknown ... probably ... inhabited till the GREAT INUNDATION towards the Close of the Fifteenth Century,

occasion'd by a Breach In the Bank of the River Thames near the Great Shipyard at Limehouse."

The great stone animals are shaken – but not, finally, destroyed; the surrounding streets crumble. The risk of the Manhattan Project is there – the way the Japanese used the sun as their totem. Future suns of blinding energy do glint in the mute pallor of the stone. Fossil forms mark the ascending steps. The systems of worship are bankrupt, the buildings stand.

To close: G. R. Levy's formulation on the Maya:

"None of the Gods of the Old Empire reached a human personality. Though partly animal by totemic assimilation, they appear to modern minds as natural energies held prisoner in time & space, engaged in ceaseless warfare to maintain their stations in equilibrium against the horror of infinity. Their expression, in an art of unsurpassed splendour, is formal & abstract, its elemental dynamism weakened neither by organic human synthesis (even where it is compound), nor by human thought & emotion."

CLOSED FIELD, THE DOGS OF THE MOON

May 13 / Monday:

Start work King George's Fields, E.3. Assistant gardener.

Interview in the office of Mr. L. Wood, the red, vein-faced, geordie boss-man; who sits on his heater, drumming well-worn heels. Child-sized hands rest on his knees, his wrists are made of string.

He discovers my next-of-kin: "just in case." He warns of "rough and ready language."

My name is on the form.

"I've been down here twenty years. They're not friendly like us northerners."

He gives me the Parks Department Manual to take home for a little light reading. It includes such nuggets as:

"7. Writing of Books. While occasional literary or artistic work is permissible, special consideration would have to be given to the writing of books for payment on subjects relating to an Officer's or employee's work for the Council."

May 14 / Tuesday:

Sun burns the neck.

Tractor-driver Ben reads an account of the death of H.R.H. the Princess Anne's horse, Doublet.

"Be better for one of us to be shot than that horse. A right shame."

May 15 / Wednesday:

Wreck my first multimower. Wrap it round a section of fence, hidden in the long grass of Rounton Road. Arthur is not dismayed. He relishes (again) the role of initiate/corporal.

Take my lunch to Tower Hamlets Cemetery.

The bothy cat, Pickle, gives birth to three kittens. Foreman 2nd Class P. Millward is putative father.

May 16 / Thursday:

Urine, milky with sperm. "Their semen is not white like other people's." Haze sky, moist air. Shu & Tefnut. The fisted phallus of St Anne's; beyond the stadium, above the railway.

This wide-sky space scale is working into the blood stream. New time vitamins. Necessarily slowing (pulse) to the rhythm of all-day in the open. Earth sucking at his boots. Cuts away from the routines (& expectations) of home life.

My intuition is confirmed. Foreman 4th Class P. Healey is a hay fever victim. His sufferings, an early warning.

May 17 / Friday:

Mugged by heavy clouded sky. Bicycle through Victoria Park to work. Uncut lushness. The white of horse-chestnut candles.

Heat bands; alternating hot & cold of diesel fumes, cruising the length of motors held at the red lights, Mile End Road. Last night's dream comes through again. An invasion of white rats, scuttling over the steps of a double-ziggurat. How to kill them? Gas, club or cannon?

The duty now is pastoral. To walk out with wicker baskets & scatter chalk-coated pellets of fertilizer over the municipal grasses, to impart that sheen, high summer greaser. Which must then be cut back. But this is easy work. I have time to look across King George's Fields at the group of industrial buildings on the far side.

Here there is money hustle. Flash cars all along the fence. Work faces stuck on expensive coats. Fur & leather bits. Fork-truck cola beans. And the leisurely shuffle of the giant dustman who works that route. Immensely slow, his pram of selected refuse. Another system, another time-scale.

For the morning session Arthur eases the landrover (never exceeding 18mph) through Ellerman Street, Lindfield Street, Sturry Street, Cyril Jackson Primary, St Anne's Limehouse, Copenhagen Place: casting the granules to left & right, wide flung arc of the arm; soon accomplished. Old Holborn rolls-up. Fluid horizontal plane of consciousness goes up in smoke.

The afternoon takes us, gently, to St Saviour's, Campbell Road, Rounton Road, & Spanby Road.

At home I plant three artichoke crowns.

May 18 / Saturday:

sits
the coat of darkness, wondering
if he would ever write it
a small
hand of light
melancholy
turkey wafer swells in his throat

in another room the electric serial
loud & raw
has taken something from his eye

"pray stick to the point"

the sentinel wood
lime, sycamore, london plane
the immigrant sails
recording night breezes
an enclosure of persecutory bulbs

the cat
is claimed is pregnant the white hairs
of fear mark my shirt
so many call
so many coffees wines

these are the summer words
& if he works
it is not all because he has to
face down
along the curve of falling energies

there is nothing more
or less
than to become unconscious

to hood this day's falcon

May 21 / Tuesday:

Clearing the junk from Cannon Street Road: grass dog patch under the protection of St George's-in-the-East. The spike gathers varicose bandages, corn plasters, blood rags, handkerchiefs, condoms, newspulp, lobotomy turban. It refuses the glass, which is taken by hand. Courage Light Ale, Strongbow, Old England (White) British Wine (coach & horses trademark), 59p a bottle, available from Westminster Wines, Ben Jonson Road.

At our arrival the guardians of this site move on. They assume a different character as they hit the street. Brown suits are pressed by deep-grain slumbers. An innate time sense saves them the expense of a wrist-watch. They slide towards the Crown & Dolphin.

May 30 / Thursday:

Lizard stretch sky. Dust pollen cuts the eye. Wind.

One of the kittens, the black, does not move. The others climb on the body. Mr Wood scoops it from the box: white flake hands. Presents it to the mother. Who sniffs it, washes it, & turns away. Mr Wood places the dead thing on a chair & goes over to the cold water tap to dilute his mug of tea. The kitten's lower limbs are still warm, the heart frozen.

At this point the dog handler arrives. Pink & soapy, with tales of the brown sex police. Insulin skin glow. Glasses set into a vegetable skull. Tightly knotted tie. Red shoes violently bulled.

He attempts to project the aura of larger fields of force at his disposal. Being part of some more massive & paternal scheme. Operates under licence of the planets. A swift tongue of lust flicks through his yarns.

He speaks of Victoria Park patrols. How the dog pricked its ears outside the tool shed. The handler sprung the lock to confront "an old man" of "about fifty-five" in company with a naked woman of the same age. She was on her knees. He was "in the act of" mounting her. His male member described a falling curve. He asked if he would be allowed to dress. "No. Out." The handler fondles the image to a near climax. As man & woman stumble into the yard. A Miltonic banishment. Fire & treacle of self-righteousness.

The handler's eye is blue ice.

He tells of rape. The dusky shrubbery. Dry earth odours. The eager beast straining at the leash. He drags "a youth" off a screaming girl of "about sixteen". The seeds of germination are cast fruitlessly onto the ground. ((To bring forth a holy fountain? Or new plant form?)) No charge is made. To the disgust of the handler. "He's my boyfriend."

Arthur & Ben munch on hunks of cheese. Wood snorts in one nostril. Peter Millward rapidly sifts the *TV Times*; he has no television set, but likes to trump the men's morning reminiscences. Ben goes over the *Sun* with a magnifying glass to locate the winners, who must declare themselves if he concentrates long enough on these columns of newsprint. Arthur, with an eye on the bothy clock which now signals the end of the tea-break, prompts the handler to one last effort.

A standing couple. Varnished by the serpent lights of rush-hour traffic. Three yards onto the turf. Woman keeping look-out over the man's straining shoulder. A centaur of darkness.

These urgencies. Sharpest imperatives & oldest instincts are broken into. Citizens privileges upon their own ground are destroyed. The open lands are chained & bolted. The handler pets & fondles his wolf.

At the end of the day the cat is gone. The dead kitten is still on the chair. Mr Wood offers his humour to Pat the groundsman.

"Go on, Pat, confess it. You put your spike in her."

Which Pat has actually to deny.

At home the blackfly have invaded the broad-beans.

June 5 / Wednesday:

Joe returns, eager to join the workforce. A toe, severed by the Flymo, earned him a few weeks at home. But he can't take it. Back to the bothy society, limping.

The boss-man does not enquire after his health. It is as if the corner seat had never been vacated. Joe notices the kitten shit in the crack of the floor under his chair, but does not move. Puts his cap in his pocket, unfolds the *Mirror*.

A telephone call has pushed the boss-man into an angry monologue. Cardinal Heenan's visit to the Borough is the excuse for some fancy grass-cutting.

Wood dredges all the bile & phlegm & domestic pain that he can muster. All the poor food & weak tea.

"Fuck 'em, the cunts. Let the Irish fuckers die. Hunger strike? Let 'em fucking die.

Cardinal Heenan? Piss on him. Let the fucker go to Ireland. Let him go on hunger strike, the pig.

They're all the same, those fuckers. The Pope's never set foot in Ireland. He knows what would happen. He'd be fucking shot."

We drift out, back to the peace of the landrover.

Joe settles himself, selects, & lovingly undresses, a toffee.

"If Heenan walked into the bothy that bastard would kiss his fucking ring."

THE WHEEL OF HIS DAYS

the sunset is sand on the floor of the lightbulb
it is earth but does not grow
        he found
no print of his skin upon the beaten grass
& the blade that bruised his nail did not
edge the meadow
                        a wire fence
holds in some of the rubbish

"let's get away from this kind of high flown language"
worries the man with the uneasy eye

        he can't
keep his mind at rest   it pains him a fever
going against the tide is refreshed
by even these sidelong glimpses of water
as we drive through Cubitt Town
towards the bridge
                        back

●

within sunlight, adoration;
bird chisel
(vibrato), a
watery brand .

also the cat vein ticking in the throat
another morning is already present with its slight
mysterious differences

it is so connected we share all
symptoms & meanings,
bicycle wheel spins
a wobbly mandala;
this is pivot
to a chain of phasic dental disasters

the polythene flag flies away on
a bruising wind that is dug from my heel

soil poultice retains warmth, on we go

blood-land: a method of seeing

frenzied coughing-up of carpet fur
home baked bread, damp
& cut like an embryo .
the attack
begins on all fronts
howls cries
according to the aperture of various throats

the day opens & they wail for it;
allow the radio in
bandage the ancient, early valves

cod liver,
a fast
better left unbroken
●

by the brain's small bunsen
eyes shut in a box
for one week
slide open on the black
fur gloss of mother's belly

life globes
even in this place

cutting & bruising the dull grass carpet
sage medicinal odours revive
hands weary from gripping the limit

Culpeper commends this:
"against the stitch, or pains in the side
coming of wind ...
defluctions of rheum"

vertiginous cloud brick monuments
dwarf the petty transactions of survival

the source is revealed
Bryan & Mullinger ROYAL OAK SPICE MILLS

'Fragrant spices ltd'
float out over Broomfield Street

we return to base
zoned to the time arm

worksheet filled, home

" flow'r of towns"

●

o, OPEN; trick of fingers .

shutter flashes gun oil, lizard eye
opposes the random movement
by producing the solid
earth number, 4: Wands or Staves,
cambers the ecliptic;

the topsoil, brushed by besom, hides the cracks

• rake the sandpit of dead flies
• cut off the signalling of groundsel
• find yellow surprising

the smoothed knees are raised
& the blood runs downhill, they could take out
a yard of vein, shift it to the heart shop
    they do not do it
a casting vote goes against surgery
views: *Frankenstein & the Monster from Hell*
& comes back up into the cloud to discover
a shattered patella, destroying
the fingergrip of the steering wheel
    chrome face of accusation
        African mathematics
    cattle, tse tse
        brass loop around neck, suspects
bondage, does not find it repellent

    vines climb over the antler
it will ground up; the bone tree
it will fracture; the cloud plate

beaten into submission, learns to value
the freedom of slave's time,
the burden is the master's.
break wrist
kick start the multimower

for a dole that is returned
gas, heat, artificial light, telephone
& the collection of household refuse

across the lid the threads of used incense write

●

"as for myself I cannot believe fully in my own existence ... the weather is threatening"
R.L.S.

the problem when I am
"not quite myself'
what, (not who), is
walking this road, Mile End,
so blankly
trying to make contact with
the specious
traffic-driven boulevard,
St Clement's Hospital,
bridge, trees, & sky

the other citizens of the pavement are looking,
(are they),
the paving slabs, active,
some
pressures driven down
harder onto the impacted gravel
& blue clay
that is almost stone again

they do not spare the water to break up
the school, Old Church, tulip bed
it gushes,
Arthur & I sit in the sun
he: on a school-allowance milk crate
me: on the concrete that covers the ground
my eyes are sore
we both yawn
he has two weeks due in Cornwall

only one worm in the whole patch
"poor drainage," says Arthur
does not care, obviously, for this ward

the water sound should soothe

he has a car (Ford Capri, GT)
but asks often for the time

& that becomes my function

teabreaks are calculated
the rituals pushed through

it is what we don't notice
that is worth remarking, & without insistence

●

the pain is in the northern sky
fish fires light the low horizon
        his state-
ments choke in the pipe
                                                land
        is bereft of tree signs
from the west
the wind is a rapid
                                    cyclorama

cut by grit, blind
pushes the bone on
        all blossom
                                torn clear,
we plant against long melancholy

lobelia, petunia, stock,
antirrhinum, geranium (Caroline Schmidt & Paul Crample),
the maligned alyssum,
begonia (red & white), fire-king,
salvia, marigold, cineraria

how the gardeners
hate this, would rather cut grass

it is noted, bitter
claimants, pain slips checked
& signed for
      sneeze
                  bicycle
                              Herodotus

Tower Hamlets Cemetery respite

"buried face down their songs
should not rise & offend the ear"

      the man
whom the trees did not love
makes peace kneeling with the earth worm
his small heart
                  creased

●

16
EYE

is the glyph
that indicates the secret gateway
to Victoria Park

hung from a New Kingdom-style Pontiac
Grand Prix motor in walnut
                              finish

where an imaginary jackal crosses
the elm path, without acknowledgement

TO FIND A FOCUS

leaving; the lamp standard
covers the N
giving us CROW HOTEL
(Truman's, inevitably)

spins on,
Industrial Sand, Bowater, Shell

scribbles the word signs
in the toilet hut, the bikeshed

cloud stools knit together
a dark thatch, the wind
is slow to move them on

the men stare out the electric clock
offer the shrub garden a week's notice

RITES OF AUTOPSY

The Act Of Seeing With One's Own Eyes
a film by Stan Brakhage, viewed June 10, 1974

"There's very little that's understandable to me about life, or even bearable, except the seeing of it."

Stan Brakhage (7.1.72)

Seeing it again, that cold blue procession of light, gives a sufficient measure of detachment. It is now possible to move back the necessary inches from this awful revelation of meat.

AUTOPSY: meaning "the act of seeing with one's own eyes," from the Greek. The act made in such a confrontation of the body's most deeply held fears. We move down into the very heart of the city labyrinth, breaking the first seal. Pittsburgh, metal town. It has been a physical struggle to set up the conditions for the making of these films (*Eyes / Deus Ex / Act Of Seeing ...*). Dead money is involved, funds from the Museum Corporations, grave profits. Police favours are required, the soothing oils of journalism. Brakhage has to operate with that stain & to make it work, to make the tension active.

Behind him is an honourable tree of achievement, shot in warmth, in gold-brown light of *Scenes from Under Childhood*, in blood flow, snow & water, the windows of home. The mythology was domestic and the magic white: "waiting for the grey lady to whiten in the corner." There was the control that a man has over his own life, and the lack of it. Digging deep enough into the frame to arrive at the junction beyond ease, avoiding nerve habits of vision, using the counter-muscles of the eye, being present as *Witness* where he could not remain without the camera, where he could not be still, & the camera had to drink his movements of escape, where the heat of pain printed direct, where the joy & the love burnt away the emulsion; the first birth, *Window Water Baby Moving*, the voyeur friend risk of *Lovemaking*.

Brakhage took Dog for totem. *Sirius Remembered*, his own dead animal; or himself, as *Dog Star Man*. Sothis would be the appropriate deity, dog star on her head. Fear also, "recurring dream of pursuit by dogs intending to tear me to pieces." Dogs/ priests, Irish & Ethiopian cults of sacrifice; the cave, memories retained.

Songs, serial fragments, day-to-day lyrics, the luminous stream, dense layers & repeated bathings that strip the frame of all nostalgic anchors of reference. When death is present – as with Sirius – the camera follows an animal heat-path of loss, pushing into the tall grass. It circles. It does not look through the event, it looks with it. *The Dead*, filmed at Père Lachaise, Cemetery of the East, offers the light of death, the glow of decomposition: a long way from the Allegheny Coroner's Office in downtown Pittsburgh.

Brakhage handles the film, the chemically contaminated strip, scratching the black away, that most primitive image-making process. He crushes the bodies of moths, so they are themselves, directly, the medium through which the light shines. Much of this is enacted in hermit retreat, in high country. "A man of wood," he has been called, by one who visited him.

And now, this natural man leaves the cabin of protection, the worn time-track, & takes his whole trembling bundle of asthma fears & demons to the city, to a darker initiation. He is orphan, taking on again a condition of loneliness, placing himself beyond the temperatures of domestic ritual. Three moves, deeper & deeper into the closed societies of the city. He looks for cramp. The city as unknown father, upon the table of the land. He wants, at this time in his life, an adventure at least as dangerous as the Moon Trip. This is to be a private Moon voyage, the terrain is equally hostile, equally blank. He wants to enter the enclosed spaces. To give up the illusion of freedom in movement. He is granted access to the theatres of life & death: the night patrol police-car (*Eyes*), open-heart hospital surgery (*Deus Ex*), & the coroner's office (*Act Of Seeing ...*).

Brakhage's initial idea-structure is soon abandoned as inadequate. He had intended to cut a strata down through the city, following on a notion of Ed Dorn's: City Hall, Hospital, Football, Gangsters. But the fire could not be stoked, it remained too abstract; he did not find himself in it. Another word of advice from Dorn became the key to the whole operation: *shoot first, ask questions later*. Open the shutter, like a vein, to all possibilities, without calculation, but with the deftness of long familiarity. First hand. Live. Raw. The uncooked moment. Document, not documentary. Direct, not directed. Reality turning onto the spool at 16 fps, is grasped with greedy hands. "I had such a desperate need." It is happening so fast that he cannot know it is happening. The store of diverging moments is replayed, in repose, as a different thing. The snake of time thrashing as he takes it by the tail. "The most naked fix I could manage on what was transpiring."

This is what he carries into the police-car, into the operating room, the morgue. His weapon is a new 15" lens, to be hand-held, against all printed instruction. "Your heart beating will create an earthquake in the image." You breathe with the camera. He cannot get far enough away from the action to get it in focus; therefore the lens is detached. Lens in one hand, camera-body in the other: complete control of physical rhythm. And he is in a deep ambivalence, at a 'safe' distance & also forced by the focal length of the lens/eye right up against the pulsing valves or the freshly opened skull. That Olson chant running through his head, "polis is / eyes", the Olson figure of death also pervaded the hospital.

The Act Of Seeing With One's Own Eyes was largely shot at the Allegheny Coroner's Office on a Sunday morning in the autumn of 1971.

Sunday, the busy day of weekend suicide & mayhem, full house. Autumn, the time of equinoctial danger. Murder season, days of sacrifice.

Brakhage does not use the filters that would give 'correct' colour balance, so we are plunged into a cold blue corridor, refrigerated emulsion.

We can only watch these secret operations *with our own eyes*, There is no other way of behaving. These things are hard to look upon. Their gaze is severe & unblinking. They are not intended for the uninitiated eye. It initially involves an act of will: to go against the married instinct; not to turn away. We do not have the comfort of the eyepiece to stare through, we face the whole blanket of the screen wall.

What occurs?

The rituals are casual, conducted without sentiment, with an impersonal skill that is almost tender. We are seeing something old, but corrupted. Not performed in a sacred state of grace, to high purpose – it becomes, through Brakhage's sacrifice, grace-filled. What price does he pay? There is the double risk of bearing witness to secret rites and the primitive fear of soul theft. These souls are mutilated and loose, scattered. They give off the poisoned light (heat) that translates impulse into image. We know about the photographs of fields that kill all insect life within that frame. We know of the concentration of a man putting *all* his attention & will down the tube at one moment in time. This cannot be a single-direction process. Something comes back up, is sucked, willing or unwilling, into the flat black box. The situation is volatile. The force field is purple with energy. We have reason enough for the light to quake & dance. Brakhage knows that he is becoming the Cursed Man, the mystery breaker.

These acts are close to those Egyptian autoptic rites that set free the Soul Bird & preserve the body shell. Anubis weighs the death upon his scales. He supervises the measurement.

The hands of the practitioner are his, as they slice up the dead shape. The knife "manifesting upon incision the signature of a Starre." But if they bottle the removed organs it is only to fill a police report. They are scribes to the book of the city, which remains unread.

The intersection with hieratic ritual is accidental, Brakhage discovers, or invents, it for us. His vision of the city uncovers a tradition that survives, in corrupted form: as death itself has been corrupted.

The face is peeled back, which is the individual as we know him; and Brakhage "had the immediate perception that the first masks made in the world must have been the actual faces of the dead." The lid of the skull is lifted to reveal a horn/antenna of bone. The chest shield is removed. The heart bird is without protection. The whole body has meaning, as heraldry, as code to some sterner mapping of purpose. This is not a random collage of edible & inedible matter.

The doctors are splitting the seconds of flesh, are cutting through the idea that the skin is a whole, one single garment, and not an infinite net of dividing events, operating at different time-speeds, knitted together in the eye, as the film itself is held by the retention of the dying image on the retina long enough to give the illusion of seamless movement. The body is a false cloak of minutes, and here it is parted, and its lies are numbered.

Information is squeezed out of the pineal gland. The affair is faster. The guts are scooped. The bag of corruptions is spilled, warm, burning up the paste of rotten meats, beers, pickles, fish, cream. Green blubber is peeled like foam. The drill smokes, whirling through bone. The enclosed chamber is thick with dispersed voices; so many lives, abrupt terminations, accidents, fantasies, deaths on the street, burst brains. Energies thrown suddenly into reverse.

Trollies glide their polythene-wrapped bundles down underwater corridors. Gaudy rags are strung around the butchered meat.

Underwear from crime magazines. Soiled vanities. Incomplete confessions, prayers, curses mix and over-lay the track.

The soul is a brief flicker of magnesium light. An illusory blue needle of flame above the chest. A lens fault. A leak of eternity. In this pit, a blade of hope.

And then Brakhage lets us glimpse the whole taint – the cigarette-holding slaughtermen in their white coats; as they dictate statistics to the recording machine. He ends with this, does not dwell on it. That is another film, another side of the story, how the coroner & the medical students "act continually ... humorous roles ... one of them said he always wanted to be Fred Astaire, and he liked to tap-dance around the corpses ..." That underbelly of ritual, graveyard clowning, savage lessons.

We notice, finally, the austere silence of the film; the muffled clubbing of the cinema door, clatter of wedge heels as R.C.A. students refuse to confront this thing further, return to their sponsored strategies.

"The eye is thine, Horus."

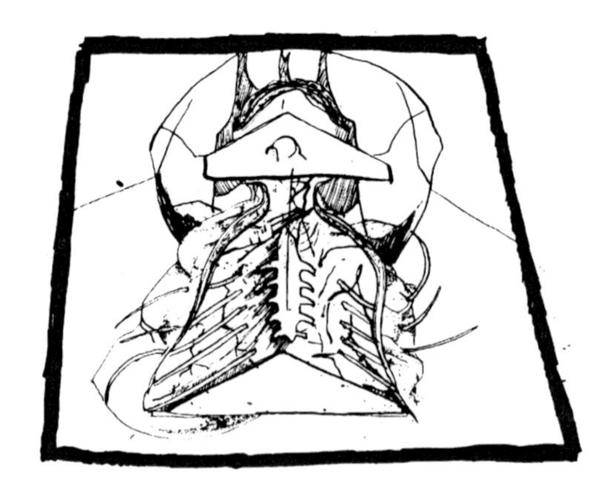

on my birthday
                    to work
      turning the prayer wheel
of the cycle
                south-east

towards the thick
      Cubitt Town
                        lingam

(this morning
      gifted with a sacrificial shirt: it can't
be worn)

                  coming back,
across the horizons of vision
      with the stone anther fountain,
                                                St Anne's

      look: with
my daughter's dungarees they give you a compass

●

the london plane
                        bouffant
drops its sticky light
hoses a segment of east city
      last rim of sun
the furnace banked down
                                with asbestos leaves
death stretch of this day
                                  waiting on
the antechamber
                        sleep
the tallest reality

"time is skin"
here to here

autopsy
dig out the soft fruit interior
paddle the scoop
– black dog –
children shout it
birds keep their heads down
"he thinks of you as totally evil"
"a con-man"
"wise"

shuffles these shock alternatives
& selects a low option

continuum of tap water
works repairs
the stem is cracked the delphinium 'dies'
blackfly decorate the broad-beans
if these are the totems of the moment we
suffer them
& gladly

●

COUNCIL PROPERTY
NOW WASH YOUR HANDS PLEASE

the hosted gaff
bladder
weakened by incursion of dandelion
& other air-borne seeds so early
(any excuse to use that word)
already
foreman 4th class (P. Healey) is hiding
his vowels behind dark glasses
& shifting to his reserve handkerchief
the enquiries of pain continue
daylong the wake of grass dust
cuts his face into a set frown

loss of egoic grip
                                        it may be
a good thing & even a passport
to Bliss Out & homogenised
7th heaven
                        "service"
has so many enfolding shades

boil the tea-dregs bitter tin
a true brew of this north island
whose existence is now un
fortunately confirmed

●

"many ... burn the veins on their heads, & sometimes on their temples, with a bit of greasy wool, as a permanent cure for catarrh"
Herodotus

picks up a piece of the jigsaw sweeping
the yard looking for a clue into this day
fearful of the mist threat
                                        the merci
less heat rays cooking all internal organs
      no mercy either
in continuing these 'spiritual exercises'
      no god is
served in such harsh & scouring self
      love
tearing the flesh in his nails along
the field margin
                              the multimower hurling
dirt in his face
      the stalks of his legs
are bruised & bruised again
      it bends to
                              his purpose

not the flesh
that is weakened arms
the colour of bacon

what is cooked out he follows
Midsummer's Day all rituals enacted
in sleep only
serves the tax machine
waters the lettuce

●

"I WANT IT"

everything that is not *here*
& everything that does not answer to
now
& everything wants this wanting
so that the lack of comfort becomes
a fixed definition
the pain is unremitting doesn't
want to bend into irony
or floods of *local colour*
won't be shifted more than two inches from the skin
can't be talked down to
coheres makes sense
he has to find the words to keep pace

it is briefly night again
sun climbs its ladder
drops on his head
it could
begin to stutter or break
into a Bergman cry for love
for the love of god
the rape & commingling
with the divine drill-head
he hopes

it's not that
        he doesn't know
what it is

all bets are covered
with an incredible system of side-stakes
& double-entry bookkeeping
        the unconfessed
use of public buildings as symbols of safety

if he can look all day
at the alternating facets of St Anne's
he is safe
                it is safe
then what did that moon dream mean
& why does he feel his eardrum
beating through his cheek
                                        why can't
he bear to sit still when his mother talks
if only it would fade
                                  into a rain dance
like that three minutes sheltering in the tractor-shed
away from the shovels of topsoil
when the waters beat out of the sky
onto the yard
& he was able
to draw breath & the murderous
calm was splintered & wind came
shoving the cloud train clear
                                          for that evening hour
"the golden hour" of Hollywood legend

        when he feels sick to be out
& goes out
                    & feels good
& feels sick to be good
                                    knowing that he must
be sick again

●

they talk about "real life"
behind walls
home is cupped in their hands like
prison cigarettes
he describes his own life
as if it were a one-day vision

in a restless dream the true poets accused him
he was late for work & took the morning off
for rapid sexual gratification
in the corridor
rolls across the floor

woman in such steady pain & panadol for two days
& nights from the knife
parents
have assumed their bed

more shit stains on the bowl after the weekend
than at any other time
how I envy
the neat fast physical descriptions
I found in that (Chris Torrance) manuscript
the dream
with the observed world is shared
envy
not the descriptions but the state of mind (grace)
that composes them

converted to ease
elasticity of vision
deepest
confession of ecstasy

*"opening up the hopefully uncensored self to the present
the fallible, living trace that is us in the world"*

A THEORY OF HAY FEVERS

"Avoid sun-or-other light, seek to travel in such a manner as to inhabit only the autumnal-and-wintering seasons, shun the company of fellow human beings, sleep as little as possible, etc. – or specifically: he must cave-live, at least as one does in the concrete city, run from the hunt of the summer equinox, avoid all flowerings, sex, laughter, or other human excitements, and rest preferably in a squatting or other wakeful position cautious to eliminate his dreams ... And so know & use "the Dark Lord" as Blake knew & used him ... as even Solomon used him to build The Temple."

Stan Brakhage (Margin Alien)

"Life when one does my kind of work is rather strange"

W. B. Yeats

What is operating here, in collapse of open-air efficiency, is a form of priestly prohibition. Red eye, streaming nose, skin irritation: are caste badges. Our bodies are wiser. Disease (greater or lesser) is a form of pure message, is concise as glyph. These summer days in length of riot & grass orgy are forbidden to the sufferer/adepts. They should hold to their rooms, they must remain in the cell of water. The sun hunt cannot seduce them from their manuscripts. They watch the boar pass, in envy. Darkness is the price of their power. Power is the measure of their failing, as natural men.

The incapacitated foreman (4th class) adopts the ruse of smoked glass: hides the eye, the knotted vein-held boil. There might be another side to his suffering (& this whole equation) – that his self-image is higher than his rung on the ladder of reality. He talks of "O" Levels as if they were edging-irons. He savages the student, who is extra to a newsreel demonstration. He plans loftier careers, buys a Ford Cortina, photographs weddings, gets

more children. Projects himself into a new landscape. Hay fever is the anchor, the counter-balance.

These accusations go against the poet with equal force. If he is not truly "here" the fevers will nail him. The continually drawn handkerchief is drenched with his melting ego. Discursive thoughts run out of his nose, the attention is concentrated in one place. He listens to the smell that is no longer there.

Brakhage, asthma priest, keeps his eye hidden in the cool socket of his viewfinder; concentrates all pain OUT into the captured image field.

Which recalls the worst days of suffering – filming at Silbury Hill, or taking photographs of Avebury, the Ridgeway – punishment for defiling the mysteries. Thick mid-summer drift of grass seed, midge helmet, surrounds these shrines, hovering over the aquastats, spirals of protection & warning.

Other warnings are closer. 12/6/74: his black polished limestone pebble, Monknash cursing-stone, disappears from his left-hand pocket; and from the landrover, the plastic shabti figure. He had found this in the grass on his first day & had immediately adopted it. The shabti would continue his true work, while he rested in labour: "dying each other's life, living each other's death." Monotony of bodywork is release, a suspension for the looms & motors of the brain cup. The shabti could inhabit that space, keep the communication active. It was hidden in the back of the cart among the hoes, mattocks & baskets. A double-loss was sustained. He was opened up to the whole horror of the sun.

Disease initiates are forbidden the pleasures of slavery. They may not enter that world. Or they will be broken. They may not celebrate the season of fertility in the land. The May Day dances seal their door. The Green Man is a tree of blades they may not embrace. The July oak-sacrifice is their order of release: "one-eyed sacrificing priests." Their time of action is the autumnal equinox. The Irish ritualised the date of the beheading of John the Baptist as August 29; Jack the Ripper took his first victim, Mary Ann Nicholls, on August 31. These are rhythms to recognise, to accept or to oppose.

"The Adept, however, must recognise that the body with all its functions is God's own creation, & the dual polarity, the force & the restraint, is the divine formula of all creation, from the flower to the man."

The Cromlech Temple's teachings on Morality & Sexuality, as recounted by Francis King.

The fevers are a restraint & a cause of restraint: the Reichian diagnosis. What has been held down will flower in this form. Plant birth. Each disease discovering its own markings. A garden of dividing songs & repeated chants. The tonal displays of chastity.

We are punished for taking pleasure. We are punished for not taking pleasure. We are punished.

This theory goes (or does not go) equally for other classes & degrees of body text. Said Kotope to the hesitating sculptor: "you know why you stutter? you think nobody wants to hear what you have to say." Not so. This is the formulation of a mental muscle-builder, someone who has lifted his idea-structure from a Charles Atlas/Dale Carnegie confidence kit. The answer is less glib. It is to do with use of air; finding the breath for an individual score, flutes of bone in the throat. A sequence of pushes towards that silence in which THE THING can be made. The oracular tongue is bitten by snakes. It is too thick for the mouth, it curls back. He speaks with tongues, very slowly. Hesitation: as for the creature with a single strike, fatal to itself as well as the victim.

Local pains block the ease of conduct in the world. What you suffer is the place you choose to live. Do not remain victim to a solitary level of discourse. To play safe & obey the surface warnings of sickness – or to take the pain route, grasp the nettle, move into one plague after another; reach the godhead by the muddiest route. Alchemy of body particles; avoid the static

condition. The magician is born of incest, is, by definition, diseased. Suffer it.

The cure, like the theory, is retrospective. When we understand the condition it no longer exists.

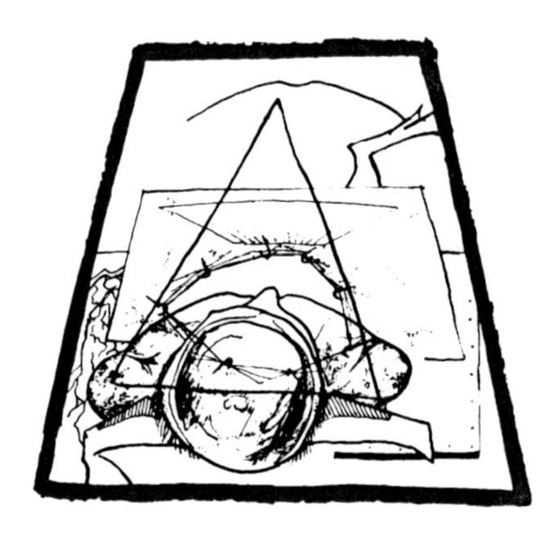

"Things which have once been in physical contact continue to act on each other at a distance after contact has been broken"
J. G. Frazer

mowing down the English Martyrs the poor
drainage & burnt grass yard of Kentucky Fried Chicken
    the nuns keep them back
behind wire
    quadrangle garages & Bangladeshi
clothing factories repress the martyrdom
bank down the fires
    resilient bents refuse to be cut
the multimower machine whines & clatters
leaves a neat impression but is not
finally triumphant
    foundation stone
laid & blessed by Cardinal Heenan

we mow further
tear across the carpet strips of Sts Mary & Michael,
St Saviour, Cardinal Griffin, St Philip
Howard & the Holy Child
all are
shaved & prepared

the steep bank
at English Martyrs is allowed to run wild
these gradients await
the arrival of steels & spikes
a wariness is apparent since Joe left
the top of one of his toes
at Sturry Street
slipped under the Flymo on the milky grass

vegetative revenge
Joe offers himself does not
voice refusal or make automatic
compensation claim
states his
fear of the long building beyond
Campbell Road
the hospice
where his mother died

"they take you in & you never come out"

low
pressure across the south lands
the clouds bruise our shoulders
but grant this pre-breakfast vision
of Limehouse Tower

the bicycle
bucks over lime roots
they have turned the tarmac apron
into a wave-sequence chart
& shake the veteran Raleigh
to its death rattle

edging
is a rest cure
carry out
the edging shears
a formal egyptian implement
"weapons of convocation"
stated the letter in its abrupt wisdom

marks of faith occur
as the bents of flesh submit
drunks in the night
push the hedge down & spew in the flower bed

I am what I have to sacrifice

●

"the citizens of London had from time immemorial used to hunt within the aforesaid woods ... hares, foxes, conies & other beasts where & when they would"

in Victoria Park the level & type of perception
changes
is no longer so persecutory is opencast
as if the forehead was cut away
& the breeze of the tree enclosure
played upon naked brain wires

the thing
here is that all messages come direct
in natural metaphors
the seed mace
of the chestnut rolls over the palm of my hand
its small
spikes touching the near-surface nerves
falls
to the ground

or the coke heap
picked out with russet leaves
        again the chestnut
long slatted mask face

        wind is
a wall of protection
does not drive against the skeleton
                                        nesting birds
dive for scraps that can be found

so everything encourages
a system of notation that could easily
be described as
                    an optimistic world picture

we are here briefly to dump a hawthorn hedge

●

the jacket is buttoned
but the hands
warm to their task
                        slide
along the rake handle
heat the primary basin

combing dry grass hay into mounds
good work
            a field of birds

angel of protection alights on the tenement

it is a field of memory
out of reach
drawn up through the prongs
as the rake drags over the ground

earthed impulses fire our tendons

we cannot see
the river beyond Lime Kiln Wharf
but Joe tells us this was
the Limehouse origin
                                        where Stow
speaks of Lymehurst, or Limehost

domed Greenwich comfort
out of reach in the Land Rover
                                                    speed
of playground

when the page is utterly replete
                                                    I'll move on

●

BIG MEAL

her legs go upwards into eternity & well
out of focus
                    the red buttons
are stages distinct as f-stops
        look how the full
moon becomes an area strongly linked
with the horn antennae of this snail
crossing our path Keats Grove
        sublime
bedroom preserved
                                the tiles of lung
blood confirming the pure status
of his quotable formulations
                                        the cases
of preserved emotion

we can look
with a whole body of lust across the table
the libidinous plates the Upmann cigar
& german wine
                        the lies
shield a condition of secrecy that needs all
his five-litre cunning & is the holiest mood
he can summon in the heat of
the matter between them

they wait on
a cold platform it does not chill
the truce of love the modular basket
they share watching fish
                                    in an air-
hosed tank
spending money free
as the bubbles break the longing
between them of the ancient dead
generations to mate again
                                        & be born

FROM CAMBERWELL TO GOLGOTHA

A reading of the double-chamber presented by the sculptor, B. Catling, at the Royal College of Art, June 1974

"I have described his ideal of beauty as thrice vomited flesh"
W. B. Yeats (journal)

"And in the Shadows of Remembrance & in the Chaos of the Spectre,
Amalek, Edam, Egypt, Moab, Amman, Ashur, Philistea, around Jerusalem,
Where the Druids rear'd their Rocky Circles to make permanent Remembrance
Of Sin, & the Tree of Good & Evil sprang from the Rocky Circle & Snake
Of the Druid, along the Valley of Rephaim from Camberwell to Golgotha,
And framed the Mundane Shell Cavernous in Length, Bredth & Highth"
William Blake (Jerusalem : Chapter 4)

To begin with the specific occasion, an exhibition (in every sense) of final works, at the Sculpture School, Royal College of Art, visited twice: June 10 & June 15.

The ground impression is obviously depressing; enclosed, cunning, banal & proficient. Our seduction is attempted. There are cries for love. Gambits & ploys are made in the force field of what-is-expected. No hand of guidance. No austere master/ disciple relation. No stern apprenticeship worked out. Welfare state feeds its woolly victims to the media wolf. A spurious search for 'originality' has been encouraged: we are surrounded by congealed examples of manner, framed gestures. Content is a starving zero. The whole thing bends respectfully to the industrial & the most 'impressive' items are the ones that are charged with some degree of self-recognition: smooth machine

artifices, skilled constructions. These are a small measure of the soul of the time. They earn a degree of respect, even though they suffer from the need to charm us.

It is within this poisoned context that I encounter the Catling zoo. The man is obviously out of sympathy with the essential strategies of the institute, yet does not oppose them with the kind of bitter & repressive fury that is, finally, self-mutilating. He doesn't waste his energy. Prepared to work undercover he gets on with it as far as is possible in this sponsored, other-directed, environment. So there is a strain that pulses in the neck and causes the eyes to bulge.

The first claim is that he uses the totality of the room as his own place. It is not a store-house of accidents or any kind of shop window. We swallow the taint; the pathology is not the true interest. Avoid the art fanciers who stroll through, fondling the merchandise & getting their claws into a piece of the future.

Along the walls are monochrome line-drawings. I read these as dedications to the necessary gods, compressed strokes, king lists, pages from the book of self-invasion; disease slides, protected by glass. They relate fiercely to earlier sequences, but are further down the track, the line is hotter, the news faster. There is sharper nerve, teeth in the sand. Detail sows the eye into a labyrinthine chaos of arrow lines, highly energised black wires that cancel their opposing thrusts: so that the total effect is a frenzied calm.

The contours have been borrowed from Upper Egypt; pyramid metaphor is active. The autoptic instinct is a genuine concern; we meet again that skull-horn glimpsed in Brakhage's film. Dissection by blade-pen reveals the processes of dry weather, the testament of the white ant. Catling discovers what is 'Egypt' in himself; relevant to his carriage in this city.

We are close to that image, mentioned elsewhere, of the astronomer's rib. The parable speaks of a Star Watcher – his night eye fixed lustfully on Saturn – he is drawn down the tube

& out into the heavens – it is that Brakhage ambivalence again – on a cosmic scale – quivering close-up of the planet's pores at a distance that is measured in light-years – the motor is an implacable hum, as telescope hungrily tracks the heat of the desired object – flame of excitement, the opening of *Prelude: Dog Star Man* – astronomer's brain-cup crushed against the curved wall of the dome – vision, at that moment, spurting into the star field – cold sperm. It is happening here: the eye is harpooned, one of his ribs breaks free, dipped in indian ink, traces the pressure makers on the revolving drum, the Aneroid Barometer. The bone needle moves mechanically. The message is remote, & the blood of this satellite, if leeched, would be malarial & white.

Signs, half-understood symbols, made fast enough to avoid the censorship of the technician's hand. Limits. Of flesh & of rock. The Man/Beast/Plant forms of the earlier drawings are not much in evidence. Life is implied. The hybridization of landscape is gentler. The obsessions are disguised by a higher need. The fences of pubic hair from the crashed aviator no longer measure the fen, the swamp. Helmet & bandage of deep sex-wounds are in retreat from the chalk dome. It was too simplistic a formulation; close to art-school desire for shock effects. Here, land is not in drag, not dressed up, & not insulted. These plates are mirror windows, compress & extend the detail that cannot be layered into the sculpted objects.

We move from these essentially literate concentrations to the floor of three-dimensional shapes. The room is crowded. The individual items so powerful that they fight for survival with saurian relish. Flapping polythene sheets across the windows mute the light & knit a reedy ethiopian wind along the border of consciousness. This is the tower flute that we meet again at St Anne's, Limehouse, standing at the foot of Hawksmoor's original staircase. In darkness we listen, on the stone flags of the south-facing porch.

The wood reach of the room soon contrives the mood of a countrytown museum; or, specifically, the feel I get in

Dorchester, the following February. There was in that building a wall of man-traps, & they were staggeringly close in kinship to some of the iron-forged forms in this chamber. They hung, gross insects, on a white wall, above a wooden platform in a long galleried hall. They were removed from pheasant grass & woodland, & exhibited. The intricacy of their construction goes beyond functional necessities. It is the same here. These beast/machines do not discover their active purpose in this place. They are charged with a high energy potential: but it is hard to tell what actual work they do. The obvious danger is narrowly avoided – non-exercise of muscle – to become greased gladiators that are not summoned to the circus – to be Samurai armour, uninhabited – to be dreadnought posture, May Day parade.

A further insult that might be offered is "Medieval Craftsmanship". Dorchester Museum again. Brotherhood of iron. The metal of Los, of cruelty: weapons, whips, the spindle of destruction, the plough, chains, fetters, cunning contrivances of the Inquisition, abattoir skills, Templar repressions. Craftsmanship that serves the butcher & the fanatic dreamer; or the craftsmanship that is deeply & truly local, ritualised, day-to-day, forging of the tools of work, the implements of survival. Membership of a traditional & anonymous guild of honour. Wayland the Maimed. It goes all the way back. Casting of magic swords. The bellows, the cave. The strongest forms discovered & passed on. No time to admire the 'workmanship' before the jaws snap across bone.

Dorset goes deep. The shadow patterns of the winter solstice yield further insights into the sculptor's vision; as he has trapped it in these plates & constructions. What he maps by loose-wrist improvisation is as accurate as an eye-copied & over-lit linear description. The shaved contours of Eggardon Hill where the chalk gives way to clay & lias are a part of the rope of energy that Catling has schematized. Meaning is defensive: massive enclosures, works of earth – that natural use of the pulse of the land. The traps: false walls, pits, mazes, tunnels, caves, ovens, burial chambers. There is a deep relation here. I am moved by an active interplay of generosities, exchanges of code, the tenderness with which Ridgeways are brought across the bones of wood, the straps of leather.

The larger dramas of these lands are not, superficially, present. No tapestry of battle, or reference to king-myth; no heraldry, no nostalgia for "mysterious britain". Direct translations of cultural collision, the point of impact: the ballista bolt in a section of spine. Iron has grown into bone to breed a new creature. This is colonisation of the most intimate kind, possession that demands an absolute sacrifice of self; a new thing is made by a violent act that becomes, by the strength of its need, loving.

The eye/hand relation is brotherly. The sculptor is at ease constructing an oven or beating out a ritual weapon. The incantations he chants are the natural sounds of these hill ridges. He prepares the feast, selects & kills, cures the meat, with the same precision that he used to forge the cauldron. Seasonal rhythms – death, sacrifice, inhumation, re-birth – are understood & coded into the machine.

"To respect the vegetal powers"; the injunction from *Rock-Drill* is obeyed. The vorticism is implicit. It is not the vorticism of Gaudier-Brzeska & Epstein – but there is a kinship with the metallic coldness of Wyndham Lewis – the idea of wholeness; that the made objects fit into a universe created by a single generative force, or group of forces that remain in sympathy – architectonic wholeness – total invention – not single small valued isolated artifacts, but a sense that the sculptor has managed to realise one detail from a whole that goes to the horizon & beyond, stratified, inhabited, furnished with building, beast, plant, star, insect – the agent & the sofa come from a single city – the gigantic architectural projections of Lewis' *Human Age* trilogy or the under-ice labyrinths of H. P. Lovecraft – approached with a seriousness that continues to frighten the casual viewer greedy for sensation & eye-orgasms – all or nothing.

The muted sadism of these forms is unrepressed. The man works from the moist heat of the body. Body/armour is the continuing metaphor. Enclosed in a protection of limits. This is crucial. It is something he had the instinct to cite in a catalogue note/ parable. The notion of power objects buried, unseen, within the mountain. Not made for exhibition. Interest in the containing mass. To sift detail is an academic neurosis. It is all here in the coastal ridges of Dorset: burial chamber stones heaped over with earth. The horizon is the polished eye of god. He aims for the time "when man shall wish the coverings of Mountains, not of monuments, & annihilations shall be courted."

And I am in the grasp of these lands when I receive, from the sculptor in the city, an account of his visit to St Anne's, Limehouse. He calls it "The Labyrinth of the Jackal."

7 February 75 *DARK PULSE. THE CANOPIC LUNG*

"Visiting St. George & St. Anne. The ratcliffe cloudform matted in helmet bone. usual boneyard shudder.

St. Anne's. the organ is more than the throat. it becomes a non music entertainment. dried of tone its bellows speak only in pulse.

LOWER SKIN OF THE DEAD STAIR.

Your sense of the membrane case becomes clearer it is rooted in corpse valley. From its apparent base in the vestry it crawls down further to ground level. At this point the decay is total, that white mould gums the wood together. From here we are with Lovecraft, James & Poe. The electricity cut, only the decayed husks of bulbs hanging, spider victims, blood drained bodies, dry. We find two candles (pale yellow, age). This virus light held high guides us.

There is a careful straining of motives, then I enter. The lower room is trenched with boxes it is an obstacle course. The boxes contain wooden balls (tennis size), trunks of chipped & dented enamel plates, remnants of lowlife feeding. Inch of light crawling in under barred metal shutters.

We climb the dust through the crypt gates, I am sure nothing has been disturbed here for years, in places the dust & webs are six inches deep. I sink through rotted wood up to the thigh in tin plates & leather bags. It is like Abrontius & assistant stumbling among ultimate hazard.

The actual passage before us is disturbingly parallel & tall. It is about 8-10 feet wide & at least 12 feet high. The flame only illuminates four feet around us, so it seems uncertain.

There are chambers leading off from this gallery, there is a nasty familiarity, it is something like the passage in my basement rooms & cellars leading off, irregular shapes; also some of the chambers are like the maggot street hydrophobia room.

They vary from tall rooms with intersecting passages to hutches with openings only 3 foot square. For some reason I feel unsure about the use of these rooms although there is a positive repulsion on entrance and I only peer holding my candle inside."

The big structures that I haven't mentioned are the true force. They heat the fear line of celluloid horror & pseudo-myth into hieratic priest language. They discover & utilise the continuum of small room english murder rituals, sealed decors, sheds & bathrooms; the rope deckchair of Christie. These quintessential forms operate on insect-time, fire at reptile blood temperature: are very calm & poised to strike with scorpic venom.

The eye is reptile also. It moves at speed around the frames of these parthenogenetic beings. "Make him of wood / with / steel springs"; *Rock-Drill* again, the marriage of skin & metal. The sculptor, at this level, is shaman. He also serves the Necropolis. Objects are made in fear & expectation of death – with an understanding of the mutualities & relevances in Siberian, Egyptian, Meroean, Sumerian & Mayan cultures. I am in awe of these things. They are made for voyages beyond the rim of reason. Turrets, platforms. Mud on the feet, neck strains through the torque of stars: that energy. In photographs we see the wooden pyramid (orgone accumulator) that is so close to the Limehouse pyramid, & was made in advance of the first sight of it; intentional, willed, pre-vision.

We see that the platform of release (execution) is a body also. The act is unified, self-satisfying. The tree has ribs & workable organs. It has badges of steel, the hooks & the teeth. The ice of metal finish & the warm blood that is in wood. "Danger threatens from a wooden host & a scarlet messenger," was the word of the Oracle at Delphi. It echoes here.

The two most impressive items in this outer room have a tribal vitality that should have been preserved & viewed again: a raft & a sledge. ((It must be mentioned that when this exhibition 'closed' the objects were broken-up – no place for them. A fact which caused John Bellany, the great Scottish expressionist, to pound Catling's head against a restaurant wall – a justified frustration.))

"The raft / is the penalty & the cure." It is made ready for the great voyage that is death. It honours the spiney form of the fish totem: the force that is in the medium through which the raft must travel. An ice platform aimed at the sub-mythic regions of Antarctica, "the Mountains of Madness." It contains in its smoothed wood the ghost journals & water-colours of that place. The polar metals are charged & magnetic: "the compass is absolved." In plain strength the aim is outwards; it turns, imperceptibly, through a field of force.

After the raft there is the sledge. This contains the idea of kneeling, prayer. An object made for extreme margins; deserts of sand or snow. A cart that scorns the wheel. The driver is an idea, outlined in steel. The sledge will not, of course, move. The journey is mental & swift. From the lead strip we follow the metal promptings down the road of flint.

The sledge also relates most strongly to the urban hurdle of execution ceremonies. Titus Oates (the irony of that name intersecting with polar tableaux) suffered the road from Newgate to Tyburn; "was this day placed on a sledge, being not able to go by reason of so late scourging, & dragged from prison to Tyburn, & whipped again all the way, which some thought to

be severe & extraordinary." The dug-up bodies of Cromwell, Ireton, Bradshaw were also transported by sledge. The stain of ritual, the desire to place horror in a formalised context; reaching a peak with the death rites of John Williams, the supposed Ratcliffe Highway killer ... "covered with a piece of red cloth & placed with face uncovered & upwards on a large board to be fixed upon the top of a cart with murderous instruments placed on either side of the corpse before which the common executioner might be seated; the stake with which the body is to be pinned to be borne before by a proper officer." These are the implications in the shape of the naked wood.

"There is a massive steel door covered in dust, at this point it is two inches thick; it has not fallen from a close aperture, but looks like it has been flung from the opposite side of the gallery. It is now totally silent locked in this beast body, testing its very nerve. The passage turns to the left here and I realise we are following another labyrinth. It winds again at the end of this passage. There is a small entrance about 3 feet by 4. Inside it seems large & subdivided, like the rest it is plastered or whitewashed; there are two flange-like apertures at each side, these give me a total horror, they are like recesses that might contain small iron doors or blades. I then enter the next turn, this passage seems less disturbed, it contains more dust & the doors are wooden & bolted.

All the chambers in this gallery are sealed. There seems to be no exit. Holding the flame above my head I see there are stone tablets carved with the dead names. On reading these I feel agitated. There is one curiosity here, it is a chamber hole about 4 feet by 3, it is about 5 foot deep & contains black or dark grey dust (soot), there are rags or bandages also, small pieces of twisted cloth. This is the most tainted thing so far and we set back.

This place is also like the pyramids the isolation here is total and with candles it even looks like one of those early prints of the discovery of the king's gallery.

Dead geometric persistence. What the masonry holds beyond decayage. Compressed, the fear of form."

The absolute spine-driven condition is achieved, as is appropriate, in the inner chamber, or shrine. This is the final statement. We enter a secondary (disguised) door & escape

from the museum/zoo society. The light is dim, twin bulbs, incinerated moth brains: so the impression of oracular wood pronouncement forms its outline slowly. There is no fear of this. Here function is realised. There is no question of the construction as a mere exhibit & it could not be sited other than where it is. It is place. The object & the chamber are truly one. We have ascended into the heart of the mystery, pushed through the valves of muscle, and seen the impurities burnt off. I am deeply moved, stirred, activated, by the rays that surround this catacomb. It is something to carry back out to the Limehouse fields: the stillness & the bandaged light. No other demands are made.

What is achieved here can probably be put as high as "a manifestation of the divine ... by mutual consent" – the form calls up the divinity – is strong enough for this function – the light is "not merely a token that the place is frequented by a God, but a permanent pledge that in this place he consents to enter into stated relations with man" – the true oracle. The sculptor opens himself, through the shrine that he has made, to divine or demonic possession – it is as risky as that – in the way that the church body (Winchester or Limehouse) is opened to penetration by the godhead – the needs are sexual – consummation leads to madness.

We are reminded of the fact of the sculptor's visits to Malta, the Hypogeum, Tarxien. An island marked by Coleridge's presence, his delirium & post-synchronised suffering, the speedy journal, the attentions of his spectre. This present shrine is derived from the condition of those megalithic caves: tomb & temple.

G. R. Levy speaks of these places: "It seems possible therefore that these edifices were erected as bodies of the Gods, their habitation in the Egyptian sense, by which the form called up the divinity."

Risk is here that is not apparent in the smoothed finish of the language outside – rough bandages of plaster cover the elbows &

corners – "mummy truths." He would work with a paste of bone. The rites, at this stage, are so close to Brakhage's autoptics. Orphan-asthma is common ground. The triad is acknowledged – the sacred 3 that Steiner noted of the Templars. So the light does come through, & is made. Shattered bone groupings, directional quiverings of the detached spine, translated into metal syntax. Splints of wood. The Hospice. The temple is erected along the path of wound & amputation. The sick crouch in their narrow chamber of incubation. Access is granted. The body of the priest is become the object of his making. The message is received in silence, & not to be repeated; it is given to him who receives it.

"Sense of pleasure we may well
Spare out of life perhaps: and not repine,
But live content, which is the calmest life:
But pain is perfect miserie, the worst
of evils, and excessive, overturnes
All patience."

John Milton

we come out of the cycle of pains
or
the pains become by repetition pleasurable
are worn down
& go into the butter
of a fat new moon

it can't change any more than
the faces of the playing cards the gradual
fading
of the carpet that is eaten away
by sunlight & fails
as our eyes fail
beyond measurement day by day

the new
mornings are prepared in sleep & spring no
surprises
dreams are sleek now filled
with pasturing delights
with round words
gentle landscapes
the sofas are human
& enclose every vertebral ache

to persevere
as the writer said to keep going
include the sick days the clouded
sequence

to come through & be content
to sink to drown with a closed
mouth

we loll in the pleasure of it
until that becomes boring & the eyes
ache again for images they cannot bear

•

"staying beyond reason"
the thing
that made americans godlike that worked their
destruction
the quality of these temples
lying white on the lap of the city
it is necessary to will their downfall
that they be born again
the flamelike
maggot rules this chest
shooting out
the eyes of the dead

"we're too many / & not enough"

John Ford no geographer
all landscapes Monument
all weathers
the Valley
the gathering rivers of death or rest
"medicine country"
skull rocks
wind
speaks the language of the tribe
a language
we do not learn

we think of the end &
plan our shots
cut our visions
in the tube out from the heart of darkness
Abbey Theatre tableaux
sculpts the
rictus the fixed emotions

nothing is
totally drained of meaning
we become
vague as John Wayne can never be vague
we abandon the quest
doubt ourselves our fathers
reach for the weapon in suicide also
are not
finally generous
have no decent sense of when the picture is over
& it's time to walk away
we allow
the weather to master our tenses
we bleed

into our boots
wail
when it does not hurt
ambiguous
counting the hairs on the brush

the city is not like the Searchers
strangers
rush the frame & clutter the composition
if
there are scars we disguise them
where the old gods are they do not remain

with Llewelyn Powys:
NOW THAT THE GODS ARE DEAD

●

"the second was that of Origen, That GOD would
not persist in His vengeance for ever"
    Sir Thomas Browne

picking up on that unlikely hope

what is hardest to swallow
is that the moment persists to eternity
flesh clings like a wet poster
  & does irritate
contrive small tortures
          demotic
boils & lesions

the healing of the soul is therefore postponed yet again
  we let
the Yoga lessons wait & the Divine Light
remains in East Dulwich
  you mock
at your peril

  plan a walk
avoid Origen's excess of faith
  there have
been darker months
         we
break open the bones to light our way
can we save enough to pay the surgeon

  the pages
of his script
      are individually handed out
we stumble through
         "walk on by"

●

Saint Swithin's day
                                        vaticinal
russian stout & tentacles
crawling out of his shaken orifice
        / the sky's
a wretched audience, slates him

Hawksmoor's Tower of the Winds has much to answer for

        despite all these doomy props
        his spirits are high
        vows to practice his breathing
        not yet ready perhaps for "the knowledge"
        but willing to continue the search

        coughs up a range of blues & greens
        that Klee would have envied
                already
        the leaves are falling
        water remains in the felled beech
        giving a false luxury

or Joe reports the decay of his lettuces
        rained out
soft at their hearts, brown leaf
        dead on the stalk,
a diet of radishes flushes him

Charlie wears the shingles cap to unblock the drains

        Tower Hamlets dustmen are on strike
        rats scale the south downs rubbish
        two stray cats shelter in the hopper
        we're talking about tv cholera & playing crib

rain beats on the roof, industrial claims are in
        the foreman
waxes sentimental a Barnsley Christmas with his dog
frost & the brass band playing Silent Night
        you won't shift far

in a single generation, the programming is too tight
the wounds respond elastically

    the ambition remains
to construct a more generous sentence

●

3 birds
a flying wedge
translated into the white triangle symbol
painted on the gasometer

recognise the augury
do not know what it means

the colours all in sympathy
    grey base
whispering greens loaded with lime
    mossy roofs
blue serials banked out

prepare the rain case
the velvet-
    lined casket
pinch the growth tip towers
the overstated architecture
    feel
the cockhead crackle & spit

axial itch point

the clue is buried in stern flesh design
complete before seed breaks out of earth

sitting upon the red obelisk
Tower Hamlets Cemetery

"j'ensevelis les morts dans mon ventre"

"THE VORTEX OF THE DEAD! THE GENEROUS!"

"For strange it was not that he should sometimes dream of the dead whose thoughts are always upon Death"

Sir Thomas Browne

At this time the work force is swollen by seasonal labour, mixed motives & rumours of other worlds. Many seek the comfort of these long skies; the 'lifers' speak of earlier visitants – jockeys, lay preachers, Orient footballers, Scots students cooking Chinese lunches. So the landrover interludes stretch & the quality of our rest period alters, acquires a new animation. Our twenty-stone opera star has to ride shotgun, his bulk & volume preclude him from the back benches, where Joe is at home, flanked by the sculptor & the narrator.

The intensity & commitment with which Arthur rolls these sites, his old Holborn, between his fingers is broken into by Charlie's desire to demolish all irrelevant architectures with his decibels; his "top C" has the added advantage of lifting skirts.

Arthur is seduced by all this grotesque bonhomie into releasing a part of his interior vision, his illuminated codex, which is a list of meals, food replays, steaks, salads, scampi risks, restaurants, roads, nights-out. Joe remains aloof, hoards his more esoteric treasures, the Japanese years & the European holidays. But now, under soft prompting, he connects us to the pouch of local legend.

The sculptor draws him out, & Joe remarks upon our habit of ecclesiastical lunches, Bede picnics: St Anne's // Tower Hamlets Cemetery, the obelisk // St Dunstan's. It is of St Dunstan's that he speaks.

This is an old centre, in urban fade, now locked & abandoned by the westward drift of social powers. Dunstan's is the church of the voyagers; the register of all births at sea. It is the church of the drowned lands (the 15th century crack in the wall at Limehouse-hole inundated 1,000 acres – there were dykes on either side of the Mile End Road as recently as the 18th century); protected place upon the great fen, the Nomansland.

The church took its name, & some measure of its power, from Dunstan, the Glastonbury reformer, who rose under Alphege's patronage to the Bishopric of London &, finally, the see of Canterbury. Dunstan has a concealed or disguised meaning, is a lapsed symbol, where "every symbol is an invocation" (Yeats). He is metal-worker, alchemist, & bearer of west country grail-force, water-light. He was a chalice maker, the Ace of Cups is in his hand. Home tells this in fairy-tale code:

"The legend of St. Dunstan relates many miracles of him, the most popular of which is to this effect: that the abbot, as the fact really was, became expert in goldsmith's work; it then gives us a story that, while he was busy in making a chalice, the devil annoyed him by his personal appearance, and tempted him; whereupon St. Dunstan suddenly seized the fiend by the nose with a pair of iron tongs burning hot, and so held him, while he roared and cried till the night was far spent."

Dunstan helped to create the notion of Glastonbury as alchemical seat of earth magic. Elias Ashmole, in his notes to the *Theatrum Chemicum Britannicum*, states

"It is generally reported that Dr. Dee & Sir Edward Kelly, were so strangely fortunate, as to finde a very large quantity of the elixir in some part of the Ruines *of Glastonbury Abbey, which was so incredibly* Rich *in* vertue *(being one upon 272,330), that they lost much in making* Projection *by way of* Trial, *before they found out the* true height *of the* Medicine."

The content of virtue is translated to Stepney. St Dunstan's is an enclosure of light, a counter to the muddy hymns & saturnine autopsies of Limehouse & St George's-in-the-East. Dunstan was only one of a number of figures who forged the polar connection between the west of England and the eastern border of this city. He carried a slower and more deeply mined time-pulse. There is a curve of optimism that he represents. The other obvious example in this field would be the Montacute/ Waltham Abbey connection. M. R. James relates the experience of the Montacute smith who was

"thrice warned by our Lord in a vision to dig on the top of St Michael's Hill ... He took the priest of the place and others with him, and when they dug they found a great stone which split and disclosed a crucifix of black flint; under it were a wooden crucifix, a bell, and an ancient book. Tofig was absent at this time, but he came back, and by the advice of the priest put the flint cross, the bell, and the book on a cart drawn by twelve red oxen and twelve white cows, and named various great english sanctuaries aloud. The animals did not budge until Tofig, in despair, said "Waltham." At once they took the way to Essex and finally stopped at a hunting lodge of Tofig's at Waltham. Here he founded a collegiate church or abbey, which Harold afterwards established as a house of secular canons."

Dunstan's Stepney (Stebunhithe, Stibenhede) was an isolated but dominant parish on the eastern approach-line. Colet, whose name is still bolted into the area, was based here; & was visited by Erasmus, who wrote: "here you find nothing but bounteous gifts of nature & saint-like tokens of innocency." Their debates put grace into the soil. It was an island of right-

handed vitalities. Exotic birds & beasts were noted within the circle of trees. Some high level of protection & illumination had been purchased.

Stow speaks of this:

"I find also, that in the month of May, the citizens of London of all estates, lightly in every parish, or sometimes two or three parishes joining together, had their several mayings, & did fetch in Maypoles, with divers warlike shows, with good archers, morris dancers, & other devices, for pastimes all the day long; & toward the evening they had stage plays, & bonfires in the streets. Of these mayings we read, in the reign of Henry VI., that the aldermen & sheriffs of London, being on May-day at the Bishop of London's wood, in the parish of Stebunheath, & having there a worshipful dinner for themselves & other commoners, Lydgate the poet, that was a monk of Bury, sent to them, by a pursuivant, a joyful commendation of that season ... beginning thus:

'Mightie Flora! goddess of fresh flowers, –
Which clothed hath the soyle in lustie greene,
Made buds spring, with her sweete showers,
By the influence of the sunne shine.
To doe pleasance of intent full cleane,
Unto the States which now sit here,
Hath Vere downe sent her owne daughter deare.

Making the vertue, that dared in the roote,
Called of clarkes the vertue vegitable,
For to transcend, most holsome and most soote,
Into the crop, this season so agreeable,
The bawmy liquor is so commendable,
That it rejoyceth with his fresh moysture,
Man, beast, and fowle, and every creature' etc."

There was also the Ratcliffe (Red Cliff) connection, the direct passage to the Thames, the World Ocean, the way out, the original landing-place. The church tower was seen from the river. Flags & fires carried away on the tide; last badge of hope to bear out into the stream.

The plague years started the burial of fear; the dark overlap. The garden was filled with pits of the victims: black compost. A boundary mark surrounded the church wall, but the rest of the ground was given over to the taint. August & September were the death months. 72 a day in the second half of August, 1665. 95 a day in September. The script in the death book changes as the Parish Clerks join the heap.

Remember that Los took this route.

"Fearing that Albion should turn his back against the Divine Vision,
Los took his globe of fire to search the interior of Albion's
Bosom, in all the terrors of friendship entering the caves
Of despair & death ...
Walk'd difficult.
He came down from Highgate thro' Hackney & Holloway towards London
Till he came to old Stratford, & thence to Stepney & the Isle
Of Leutha's Dogs, thence thro' the narrows of the River's side,
And saw every minute particular: the jewels of Albion running down
The kennels of the streets & lanes as if they were abhorr'd"

Joe is grown from this territory & carries the harsh splinters of childhood incident as a warning against excessive demands on the current material rump. And Joe tells us how he had been assigned to work this enclosure, St Dunstan's. In righteous awe & respect of the old tokens, the books & the windows, the memorials. It was his pleasure & his duty to speak to the visitors who re-crossed the seas in ancestor pilgrimage. Until the incumbent cut across this. Refused to unlock the doors outside certain hours. Until Joe was summoned back to work from King George's Fields, to accept the Stadium as totem. And the fortune of the parish fell with the putting out of that beacon.

It had come to Joe, along with a summer casual & wildman, young Johnny, to clear the old sepulchres. To rake off the topsoil & dig into the earth. The stones were needed to make flower gardens. The ground rental was not to be renewed.

Joe, the fall-guy, stumbler/survivor of the triads, drove his spade too hungrily into the turf & dropt through into the vault. His feet going down among rotten wood to crush the bone skeleton powder. His fear was authentic: "goose pimples like golf balls." Kneeling on the dust sternum.

Young Johnny was the other thing, no tenebrous spinal awes, no scruple. Savage eye for the main chance. Nomadic & sudden; food-stained overalls cover his pyjamas, a cap pulled down tight on lank & greasy hair. He crowbars open the huge lead-sealed box & chews the gold ring from the bandaged bone hand. And carries it back to the bothy for closer examination. The vibrant aura of Joe's fear is so powerful that Johnny relents. The ring is returned.

A service is held for the re-burial of these bits & pieces. The commandant, Mr L. Wood, attends, his first visit to the operational front. Joe is also present, but stands off, under the trees, modest & horrified.

the light is mortal

out of the body nest

the ego is not murdered but shelters

in gardening

a chaos of plant life loosed to discover its own parliament

it is

a table of skeletons talking

father fixations

stab the bean porridge

fingers are burnt upon pancakes

no meat fuel is taken

Elk Bones

offer the dead word the message of tomorrow

on the reservation

the drums

summon old gods

our dreams mislead us

swerving through this the weather

changes & rain brings relief in the night

dusty soil drinks a preparation for cabbages

he cauterizes

the memory of these monologues with Rimbaud

don't wake the baby

his wife holds her nightdress is pink from

sleep

scribbling at dawn no work today

it is only our faults we have to offer

this is the true nature of the feast that

breaks our communion

& we no longer

need to detail the clothes the wines

this much we HAVE moved

        the cat
chases the bee drawn to the light it
is man who cannot leave it alone &
acts as his meddling nature intends
& breaks the chain
                                throws open
the door
burns us in starlight prem-
onitions of equinox
                                  mutual admiration
of the electra complex

        understand this
step is bitter & no metaphor
will explain it

proud of their wretched karma the bone lips
yap
        & fed the wise
stomach stifles its complaint

        so the
instinct must be honoured NOT
to go back
                  as the man said
unless we can do it EXACTLY
each footstep in each footstep
        or simply
recharge the present

        because here
the genes fall into the old pattern it is
sexual or pre-sexual
                                  language
is the leaf-system
one attacks another defends

the women
romance each other
all rapes
are sublimated in seizures of food

mouths filled we play it out
but the conviction wilts
the chromosomes
are snookered

Death is the fuel we are using up; its smell
not unlike petroleum. Sickness. The tree plug
drains. Sky: colour of vein tissue. Too much
melodrama, churchyard lunches. Picnic against
the pyramid at your risk.
The absurd latenight horror film is oracular:
puppet theatre truths. Charlie asks for the
names of the trees. The woman in this game
remains "on the side of life". But she's gone.
The plans to view F. W. Murnau's *Sunrise* are
shelved in hollow body collapse. Swallow the
commercial maggot &
acknowledge the respons
ibility is Mayan.
Feeling his heart
under a red shirt,
sunstroke spews up
a snakeshead. It
stares from his
mouth. The black
plans are shelved
also. Acknowledge
the heart's enlarge
ment. The screech
of unclassified gulls.
Heart does sing to be part of the fire chorus.
Consumed, standing on its legs. A spider
in the cave. A blue plastic bowl is
at the bedside, he will not be
sick. Work is a telephone
call away. Obey the war
ning in your teeth
Trust your inst
inct if you
can find
it.

IN THE SURGERY OF THE SUN

August 6

"While Manu, the Sun-Initiate, guided the more highly developed human beings from Atlantis far into central Asia, there remained behind in Europe the lowest of the low – those who had fallen most deeply into error & corruption by the betrayal of the Atlantean Mysteries"

George Adams (Mysteries of the Rose-Cross)

"The spectroheliosсope shows a further transient phenomenon of flares or eruptions. Occasionally, in red hydrogen light, an intensely bright spot may develop within a few minutes and then die away again. Such spots are usually associated with active sunspot groups. What they are is not certain, but they may be considered as gigantic explosions on the sun. When they take place, strong ultraviolet radiation is emitted simultaneously with the visible radiation; both reach the earth at the same time. This ultraviolet light affects the D-layer (one of the gas layers in the earth's upper atmosphere) and causes a radio fadeout. One to two days later, further radio interference occurs, as well as magnetic storms."

(The Penguin Encyclopedia)

His guard is dropped. He is at ease with the rhythm of the days. Joe has his week's holiday. He drinks the calm restraint of Arthur's routine across the tired grass. The pollen dance is broken. We bend towards the equinox and work the patch named "St Philip Howard". The sky is sheeted, grey-mauve. He feels the weakness enter the plates of his feet. The charge in his bone marrow sustains a field of deformed mushrooms. He can scarcely climb this humble calvary & trim the toes of the wooden Christ.

This day's alfresco lunch pushes his confidence to the point of risk: to rest with his back on the pyramid, St Anne's. The buried brain. The power socket. To swallow the can of mud water is

difficult. The greasy fish twitches in his throat. Salmon Lane flickers into white fade as they return.

By the end of the afternoon he is done. And can scarcely get the bike home. Feels/understands the true distance of this journey, the pain trail. Cut-out mechanisms are inoperative. He sees every yard. So the idea of viewing Murnau's *Sunrise* is shelved. As is the scheme, already in motion, of walking the flare-path of Hawksmoor's churches by night, in company with two others; taking drinks in the appropriate cellars & rat-holes (Old Horns, Balls Brothers, Carpenter's Arms, Seven Stars, Ten Bells, Blade Bone); flash-bulb photographs to burn a dark halo around the necklace of shrines. This outing projected for the ninth day, Sumerian time of sackcloth & ashes. This was the overload.

And what occurs is seen as sunstroke. A total collapse. Water stomach. Weak head. Fever. For two days, sleepless; his body his bed, vertebrae a cage of burning wasps.

Then the dry thunder, the club shaken, & he can climb out of the nest: It is the ultraviolet knife that forces him to confront the part of him that is Robert Louis Stevenson: "thin-legged, thin-chested ... light in ragged luck." Consumptive skin flares. Unnatural fires glowing beneath the cheek. The whole horror colour range – as with that night of chocolate-cake cannabis, when cosmic ironies stretched into coffin draperies, & his companion vomited – ritual death-mask. The Jacobite left-handed ahrimanic gruel-water magicks of Caithness are upon him. He crawls out, on the third day, shaded in straw, a photograph of the last months of D. H. Lawrence.

On return to the work sheds the men laugh – sunstroke in London in August? But the magnetic storm does confirm that ultraviolet diagnosis. The sunspot code has been activated, the radio message of the Ripper. A time of open wounds, when the clouds of protection are pierced, & the gas blanket wears thin, when "one lifts a flap of paper to discover both the human entrails & the starry heavens."

August 1885 found R. L. Stevenson in Dorchester, aiming at Dartmoor, for health, renewal from stone source – but collapsing in Exeter (New London Hotel). August 1887, his health again in balance, Stevenson shipped out, Tilbury, on a freighter (the Ludgate Hill) for America. The last instinctive search, on a Sunday, was for a copy of Hardy's *The Woodlanders*, to carry with him. The narrator discovers these facts in Dorset. He has one book by Hardy in his cupboard. It is *The Woodlanders*.

The whole fever condition is stained with the pus of the Stevenson figure. Stevenson is insomnia; the wall-prints of an exhausted brain. Hollow words echo, dream quotations: that he has to "swallow the world." Dreams suffused by "a peculiar shade of brown, something like that of a sealskin." "Afraid of the clay soil."

What does he think is the governing process here? It is a total sun surgery. He is now post-operative, convalescent. With a taste of metal in his mouth, the iron of Los. He blinks from the daze & illumination of shock treatment. There are brilliant images on the borders of consciousness, but they cannot be replayed. The spine shivers from the electric couch, sensitive to the unspoken word. A confusion of tongues & radio voices from deep space-time: the dead speak too fast. A sense of genetic bombardment. As if the pattern of chromosomes had been re-made; the DNA dial spun recklessly. This is a laser lobotomy – actual major character assassinations worked by sun knife. Jekyll dreams, Limehouse nightmares. The germicidal push. All the bacteria of body light have been boiled in malarial blood heat ((the Swedenborgian distinction between the spiritual sun – LOVE – & the material sun – HEAT: Blake's "sulphur sun")). The conviction that death is the cure. That life is a disease, living is disease, is active. Death is a bath of ice. Is the water he now wants, so indiscriminately, to drink. The cure is a piece of death. Death cures the body; its furious nerve pulse. The pages of skin are dried upon hedges. This is cosmogonic surgery: way beyond his control. The patients are not individual, are a strata that curves through the alternating times of the earth. They are beyond the simplistic butcheries of tower block hospitals, secret hotels. The thing is Mayan. Connected to the shape of the essential building, the star tower. Executions (release) are multiple. Each heart torn free from the body case is re-united in the sun. That the great tribal heart should beat. That the sun continue to burn. So we 'volunteer', are generous victims, with Divine Light grins; placing ourselves in the open air, bare-necked under naked skies, away from the safety of the enclosure. We offer ourselves to the equinoctial sunbeast; so that it does not fade, or turn away from us. That its potency is held. That it climbs from the thawing earth into the heavens. Risen arch. Light maker. Promised feast of gold.

Surgery takes effect, what remains? We stumble into the realisation of a doppelgänger principle. The feeling was already present, of a secondary personality developing, Ka assertion, inhabiting this body shell. Not quite myself today; I am host to motivations that cannot be understood. Stevenson again: "... & now suffering from what was loosely diagnosed as malaria, he had convinced himself that he had ALTOGETHER CHANGED INTO ANOTHER CHARACTER."

As the ego breaks I am host to another being, who pushes through & not with the pink tenderness of new skin – but with old flesh hard as wood. The earlier "I-do-not-know-who-I-am" virus is confirmed, as this terminal caricature eases out of my face. His disease ratio is speedier. He is further down the slipway. He offers suicide cassettes, seductive quest routes, film clips of Orkney death rituals: the whole horn pouch. He packages ancient horrors in mute jackets.

The wind is aroused to push back the hairline. So there is that shock, *Performance* re-take, of seeing this thing in the bothy mirror, as he washes the earth from his hands at the end of the day.

And worse is to follow. Another of Anna's casually recounted, but vital dreams: that there are two creatures, one is her husband, the supposed protector, who is sitting upstairs in a wicker chair, while the other, also with my face, kicks down the door. Hyle is straining his collar.

He thinks of the churches as instruments of surgery, himself as golem, invaded by the planetary beams focused by these pyramids. *Invasion of The Body Snatchers* formula. Disease is the means of inter-galactic mutation. The germ is Martian. We are invaded by a virus bearing the message of the stars. Cancer is star memory, misunderstood or opposed. Involuntary sacrifices are the hardest to make. These white conversations rip open the sluggish condition. Talk is faster than light. In the wake, the fouled wash, come the abortions: Scientology, Manson Hole Visions, the Process, Roger Corman. It is too ripe, too ferocious & sudden. He wants to bury himself in a peat bog, to sink in limestone caves for a thousand years, meditating on Conan the Freebooter.

But he has to consider the pyramid, as cause. He attributes this church to Selkis ( ) one of the canopic guardians, scorpion-goddess, identified with the scorching heat of the sun; shown as a woman with a scorpion on her head. And this is illustrated later – September 4 – at Stepney Green School, when old Bill Gates, the tea-maker with the ruined feet, came out, for the first time, with the school-gang & actually spotted (or caused) a scorpion on the path. We were sitting, dimly, on the grass verge, "taking a blow", gazing with dead eye at the talismanic arachnid as it crawled towards us. Bill was the instructor: "that's a scorpion, you watch when I touch 'is tail." Which he did, the prong arching fiercely back. And we accept this verdict, do not struggle with its meaning.

One of my proposed companions for the night walk did not escape the word of the pyramid either; was opened to receive the appropriate message. He got a varicose vein on the male member.

The sun tho' must be the final agent in this parable; must be given, even here, its fee. Remember that "Cleopatra's Needle" is, in fact, the obelisk set up by Thothmes III in front of the Temple of the Sun at Heliopolis. Consider its relation with Hawksmoor's twin obelisks: St Luke's, Old Street (church decayed, obelisk standing) & St John, Horsleydown (reduced to a mere rim of brick).

We are standing, in this cantref, on the path of the procession of the sun as narrated in the journey of Los. Los/Sol works that reversal into the infinity of mirror space: west to east, from druid burial heights at Highgate, beyond the Parliament Hill tumulus, to the Isle of Dogs (Anubis/Leutha). Blake himself suffered when he took his outings upon these local hills: pain begins at the Angel. He crossed the river to the groves of Lambeth. We honour his route.

Los works his surgeries upon Urizen, the calculating intelligence, harnessing the dance of sunspots, "... till a Form / Was completed, a Human Illusion / In darkness and deep clouds involv'd." That Reason be cut into, bound, re-forged, charged with wild light, ionized. Our mummer shadows recall this great archetype pageant. It is all there in the book of visions.

"... pale stood Albion at his eastern gate,
Leaning against the pillars, & his disease rose ...
Upon the Precipice he stood, ready to fall into Non-Entity.
Los was all astonishment & terror, he trembled sitting on the Stone
Of London; but the interiors of Albion's fibres & nerves were hidden..."

READING IN BED

the sights and sounds are muted
the text also became un film noir
as dreamt
with all the multiple complications
ironies
& shifts of meaning
variable typeface
the horror was what he got right

it was comfortable
afternoon bars
fire in the Carpenter's Arms or
working hard at irrelevant cellars
"dignity in the last goodbye" never
"money, embarrassment, paranoia" is closer

the secret routines are uncovered at risk
& the point is
that *the objective* is nonsense
& *the scientific approach* a bitter farce
unless it is shot through with high occulting
fear & need & awe of mysteries &
does not demean or explain
in scholarly baby talk
it is always wisest not to
speak ("Against Wisdom As Such") the thing
spoken exists in the world & again
takes on that street determinism & punk inevitability
of the pulped detective
knowledge/suicide
each clue interpreted
speeds the end
or marriage
if we should come through into the sunset
we will be sadder
criminals

●

SICKNESS RETURN

citizen is broken the sky is
        incorruptible
immune to selfish pleas
"less to say"
        becomes less to do
then it changes
& is changing & continues to change

his head is vulnerable
as the egg Yeats
speaks of
                the rubber egg
continually turning
                inside outside
above waves

        weather frets them
giant blackberries gather the water
& are themselves gathered
        thorns in the hand

all consolations begin here
where the image turns to sugar & we
retreat from the garden re-
tract the mood of lunchhour talks
return hurriedly from the graveyard
        load the trailer
                                rubbish blows over
erases the enclosed field

        drink we must
                                a well-formed stool
or the notebook shrinks in the hand

●

HANGED MAN/REVERSED

murderous milky calm . poisoned mother
suckles the dung flies
    on ultra-violet inks
A C C I D E N T
sculptor spills himself on the tarmac
    courts death
is accepted
that vaporous Long Man of Camberwell clouds

could the roof top transaction
    telescopic
superimposition of planetary emblems
at differing life speeds
have forced the butchered exhibit down the tube

the stars are fixed in their arrangements,
claims the madman,
    they have filled him
with depressants, anti-
                                        depressants,
    vitamins, purges,
denied his vision   as alien
    & now the body breaks
    teeth fall out, hives, weak stomach,
    varicose vein on the male member
P R O H I B I T I O N

(wretched as Kaspar Hauser)
that the mind can no longer torture the body
that the mind should be free of these muddy chains
    he is mindless, a god
the star needle punctures all remaining ego
    enforced self denial
keeps the pressure up, the clouds apart
plane spotters enjoy the clear mornings
british racing pigeons manoeuvre at speed
we eat too much icecream, too many saveloys

"afflictions induce Calliosities, miseries are Slippery"

THE IMMIGRANT,
THE SENTIMENTAL BUTCHER

"life, / with a capital F"
Charles Olson (Maximus, Letter 5)

All immigrants, but in this web, in this net of ugly brickwork mosques & God hoardings, they are mostly Irish Catholic. It is there in their names, if not their voices: Pat Coyle, Peter Healey (new immigrant, via Yorkshire fish-dock), Joseph Rust, Charlie Leahy, the keepers, soft-voiced Dennis (who returns to the West for every holiday), & Johnny Cashman.

It is Johnny who remains closest to the root tradition, lives in the family drama & brawl & loquaciousness of drink, fights, monologues, jokes, vomit on the stone steps – a tribe of sons – has solution to all the major political social & economic problems, Ulster – "now you take this Captain Eugene O'Neill,

he was the best they've had over there" – shuffling dancing music-hall, or gaff, delivery; twitching at his lapels, flicking his cuffs, spilling his eye – keeper's hat, a jaunty prop – rambles of the mafia operations of local government – hard-men, fixers – he still has the priest-whipped childhood in church schools to bring up – was there with all the big local cogs & wheels – "good old Johnny". Behind this is the memory/legend of how the Irish were pushed into these boroughs, Stepney, Poplar, Wapping – suspects & villains – read the Ratcliffe Highway Massacre transcripts – forming their own protected enclave – having to profess an alien faith & culture – keeping out the Whitechapel Jews with boot & fist – a thick vein down into the life of the place.

Arthur is the odd man out – Arthur Vinton – Hugenot – the earlier Spitalfields immigrant – with that love of flowers & small birds. Cages in windows, bird-song, work ethic, green patches among brickdust shadows: Flower & Dean Street, Fournier Street, Fleur-de-Lis.

August 5 / Monday

Arthur & I have the trailer backed-up to wheel the mowers down the ramp & cut the small patch of Holy Child – when Arthur spots an old time friend, on his rounds, in a van. They talk back into narratives of shared days, we all rest on the pavement.

The most recent drama the friend offers is the Usher Road vigilantes – who have declared war on the squatters who are trying to plant a different culture in their territory. The street is already condemned, the families moved out to new flats & tower blocks – & certain groups of squatters have been allowed to use the shell of the buildings, without rent, by the local council – homeless, feckless, tough-minded, dopers, divine lighters, sufis, on-the-roaders, professional anarchists, breakdown cases, unemployed activists are here – tho' in the main it is east end families, or women with children, who cannot find anywhere, let alone anywhere decent, to live. But the indigenous mob won't stand for it. They work & they have devoured media fear. They break in with pick-axes & crow-bars – rip out the wash-basins, tear out the light-fittings, dig up the floor-boards, hurl the cookers out of the windows, kick out the window-frames – crazy escalating excitements. Arthur's nephew has been one of these, a leader, arrested, fined – a fact that he only now discovers.

The flurry of hot images settle – they go back to the small birds & flowers – the pigeons they both kept – the dogs, their tricks. How the neighbourhood cats used to sniff around the pigeon sheds – until Arthur's friend devised a cunning trap, a water-barrel with a pivoted revolving lid – when the cat stepped onto the lid it spun away from him, dropping him into the water. Every 3 or 4 weeks the barrel would be tipped out & a dozen drowned beasts added to the compost – "you do a lot of gardening in the evenings" – the neighbours would remark admiringly, as yet another pest-hole was dug. One big tom had been cornered between them, its skull flattened with a concrete-headed hammer. The warmth of those days, recalled: the laughter.

August 21 / Wednesday

Afternoon at Sts. Mary & Michael's – where we have a friendly caretaker who brings out tea & biscuits – tho' on this occasion he is away, a holiday.

The grass is thick & lush – Arthur spots a goldfinch, & then another – near nestlings, hopping about – the mother in attendance, watching from the tree. They are almost able to fly. Involvement, suspension of all other activity. Joe & Arthur talk of their own caged birds, the Club Row stratagems, painted sparrows. The training of song birds. They are tempted to catch & keep one of these, but aware that it is forbidden. A traffic warden joins the discussion. Arthur tries to help with the flying process. He picks up one of the fledglings & throws it at the tree. It falls, he picks it up again. Then the other does fly & Arthur &

Joe share the excitement. It hops, strains, gets, briefly, off the ground. Sudden swoops.

We mow the grass. The thickness is cut back by the whirling blades. We switch to a different level of concentration. Arthur stays on the goldfinch patch, Joe does the edging. The job is soon done, ice-creams are bought, we sit on the wall.

Joe notices the first one: a goldfinch head – the small decapitated thing lying on the grass-cuttings, then another, then a third that has been cut nearly in half. Arthur feels the horror. The mother bird diving from tree to tree. The whole year's tribe has been wiped out.

We wheel the mowers back onto the trailer, & return to the yard. The day's work is completed & it is now that we notice the final bird, the survivor. It is on the trailer. Joe picks it up & puts it in his lunch-box. He stops off on his way home & returns the bird to the nest.

August 23 / Friday

Cycle past the bus-stop, St Anne's, Limehouse – to lunch in the church grounds, & notice Francis Bacon waiting there, or rather, standing there, seeming not to wait. Grey – grey shirt of pseudomilitary cut, grey trousers. We eat & then count out the 9 steps of the Osiris ritual.

If
the bodies
are empty, cloud
vapours are the spin
off dialogues; are
thicker than
speech.

We all adjust: over the stadium, the missing spire,
the half-circle of border ditch around Limehouse
keeping out the histories of Mile End, Ratcliffe,
Poplar. Laneways weighed under different gasses.

The encroaching fen. The
speed of the time of the place
changes. Now I am frighted
in retrospect by a glimpse
of the original wood:
Hawksmoor's staircase
rising from the recently
sealed porch. Unvarnished
grain of parallel universe.
There is also Hablot Browne's
etching. Strong ground.
To be here is wide enough.

UNDERSTAND THE SPREADINGS OF THE CLOUDS
THE NOISE OF HIS TABERNACLE. Endure,
listen. At the mercy of cattle replays,
open fields. EGYPT – THE UNREDEEMED.

Today Arthur
called Charlie out
to witness a double-
rainbow. I remain
in the bikeshed,
finger pores
irreversably
black.

THE NEAREST COAST OF DARKNESS.

●

subdue all ego
(& rigorous eye)
into the unmarked
morning quality of autumn light

low sun sheathed above water

and the park is
an ideal
that has been there all along

PRAISE

the thick black shadows
south-east / north-west
the grooved trunks of chestnut
london plane
which is early century optimism

holds out
the street life hard channels
traffic ditches

the affair reduced to a pulse-stopped stillness
the urge is secondary to make note

interrupted
with instruction
in how to operate the tractor tilt

then back to a second breakfast
the *Mirror* the *Sun*
bad jokes Securicor pay-packets
four kittens newborn
pink leg stalks nested in moss peat

how to drown them
nylon stockings & a brick are favoured

no action
but the carrying out of milk for the mother

to work in good heart

●

though the 7.30/8.30 am light is beautiful
it is not the optimum time for grass cutting
the dewy grass covered with dogshit
that has not yet hardened
        early bowel move-
ments & the rapidly spinning blades
flick the stuff deftly
over jacket neck face glasses
later the hazard is only on boots

        clear eye
            shadow companionship
each grass blade thickly inked in

the noise drowns the smell

        tea-break in the bothy
old Bill totters back from toilet duty
hush-puppies
                        favouring ruined feet
mashes a pot of brillo tea

cheese ryvita tomato Homer

        a mistake
that alerts the foreman
who launches into a glistening monologue
stratifying the Aeneid

the same old scenario faces us
of quarrels jealousies violence
meddling by gods
                            Son of Cronos
head-office bungles the bonus slips

nothing changes

●

the cat drinks her reflection
from the rain-puddle near the hopper
we chuck out the summer plants
Joe cuts geraniums at the joint
"chuck 'em all away the bastards"
orders the yard boss
the manager uses the landrover driver
to carry him to the doctor's house

asthma chest-cough nicotine
Election Day
soft persistent rain

inside the hopper
flower mash a fridge
on the lid a speedy
calligraphy & corrosion of painted signs

the keepers join the afternoon dig
& call a spade a shovel
& feint at a National Front vote (or 70£ bingo win)

bad economics
a fortune in fallen leaves
squandered
thrown away for tidiness
a fresh set of plant teeth

thinking back to my first visit (May)
& how this land has become familiar
& resolved
fitted to the pattern or come to terms

knowing hoping that the grace is
no state of clothing or appearance
or statement or dressing of language

but to accept & include
the distractions
the day-to-day breath & performance

the lies of the land
        & nervous
scenery of the clouds
as these showers fall we must not
yearn again for sun only & the warmth
using ourselves
                            the supply
is diminished

        a group forms
leaning on brooms
the boss-man is angry & coughing
        his use of air
he is dying faster than the rest of us

nothing to forgive

the hormone advocate is resigned
& talks of Japanese gardens
the beauties of red & gold lacquer work
'the best years' of his life
stationed at Hiroshima & Nagasaki

foliage is persistent also
                the rain-
gardens not much visited

money fear scents the ground
        the prisoners
are not scared to death
pools bingo are the survival cassettes

behind the eye
                            gentle fantasies
otherwise it is a discipline without hope
of heavenly bonus
for necessity not reward

life given
                to live
"& light but the shadow of God"

●

THE QUERENT, AT HOME

the sun splinters in the high trees
      it is local, a sign
& true source of october warmth
                                                    no hurry
      how could there be
as the child stops to pick up a stone
to tear a yellow privet leaf

(my own, earlier, nervous habit)

not drunk any longer but last night's debauch
remains in the blood stream
      how we flaked out on russian stout & cider
the sculptor collapsed in the street
                                                    & came back

the madman alone was calm
                                              no
problem: a new tweed suit, a red shirt
      bandanna
                    mother's gift,
social security cash jangling in pocket
is 'cool' almost
& considering a male model portfolio
      tells jokes

gozitan cigars knock me down
the hairs on the back of my fingers
                                                    burn
      the flesh chars
no pain   the smell of
unoiled shish-kebab

in this morning sun I notice
my finger pads are gouged & cut
the sharp blade through the green tomatoes
the onions the green pepper

  no pain no blood
so we feel inhuman
& dream of blood cancelling pregnancies
don't quite understand
  the manipulations of time
but read about them

this eyot
  the privilege
of the streets

"there are still enchanting enclosures, such as
the little group Albion Square, Albion Terrace &
Albion Drive, with fine public houses, the
Duke of Wellington & the Brownlow Arms"

  claims Arthur Mee
in *London North Of The River*

the season the walking
            out
  the child
finding pleasure in simply
treading the grass

put down the elements
  a bowl
against darker times

here: Hackney South & Shoreditch where
Mr Robin May polled the National Front's
best result   2,544 votes
mechanistic
  sanguine

cloudy engine

  love
moves the sun

●

breaking away from
to write
breaking deeper
towards it
the spread of mist
across Victoria Park

seen in nature
as in
a thousand
Hammer horrors
or Mario Bava

but this is moments after sunrise
a moistness
a chastity over the lake

opening-up the toilets
becomes a pleasure
he gapes
at the sky
flight of birds
rain belt gone over

sharp focus
flight of five
high against the bony elastic of the cirro-stratus

sunlight flashing on wing tip
all these energies
aligning ne/sw
corner to corner
across the envelope

the fire ball lifts
burns the eye blood
cornelian ecstatic over Burdett Road
roof silhouettes
lifts & arcs

the tightness
goes out of the sky
smoky vapour to cloud rust

the sun is gathering
a yellow alchemy
"swiftness, as that of an expired messenger"
push
of day reality

engines starting up
in the Borough Yard
camaraderie of the few men
stamping & puffing out
milky sleep breath
the work week opens
close the door
weather eye
for foreman
snatches of Homer

sky becomes porridge
"dispersed Seminalities"

●

THE FINISH, CONFIRMED

final day, poltergeist fury
locked wheel
oil spurt
eggshell razor
baby coughs blood

surely it can't mean
that "they" don't want me to quit

impelled
towards high places

scree lake
field pattern in the valley below

as yesterday afternoon hoeing the water-jump
resting leaning on the pole
lifting to a vulture's eye view
of stadium & self
lifting
to the noise in a gull's throat
"not to quit"

can't be the message
more probably
some final exactment
blood money
what we have is brought / to live that way?

dream sorts out the tangle
a chaos of small guilts & anxieties

Anna sickens towards the new life
the frog-bud forcing itself in her womb

register these colours

ice tracks on the pillow
death

is every mother's prophecy
Achilles not specially privileged in this

egoic stubbornness driven in by blows

only the graveyard grows wild
where Ropery Street meets Southern Grove

his fictions oppose the rain
the "Eezion" power-tool ejaculates oil

says Arthur with his usual
unexpected
perception

"I have an idea this is the finish"

RUNNING THE ORACLE

"It is only when the power of the passions is dead altogether, & when they have been crushed & annihilated in the old retort of an unflinching will; when not only all the lusts & longings of the flesh are dead, but also the recognition of the personal Self is killed out & the 'astral' has been reduced in consequence to a cipher, that the Union with the 'Higher Self' can take place."

H. P. Blavatsky (Occultism versus the Occult Arts)

"Punt's Establishment was a Moon God or a Magus of the White Planet, indicating that he was a white man. At least two shrines to Al-Mukah exist near Axum, one being at Yeha about ten kilometers to the south. Al-Mukah seems to have been the patron deity of the Island of Meroe & of the Island of Ireland. His southern shrine in Meroe consisted of a small rectangular building about nine by seven metres. It contained cylindrical & cube-shaped incense altars & a bench which stood in the eastern part of the temple. On this bench, archaeologists found a votive plaque stating that:

two persons GRB have consecrated to the god
Al-Mukah the work of their hands for WRN.

The sanctuary dates from the fifth century B.C."

Winthrop Palmer Boswell (The Snake in the Grove)

The year begins with a rush of blood, pent-up force of work months, stored earth rhythms, cortical projects, margarine sentimentalities bleaching into "vision" – breaking out now into road frenzy. A salty thirst for holy places.

He departs on the last day of the dying year, north: Ripon Cathedral, black moss castellation & furious wind, calmed a few miles across country at Fountains Abbey, water park, false time zone, ruin. And the push continues; the new year opens on Holy Island, a meeting arranged at the arch, the bent bone of illumination, site of pre-birth manifestations. Totems carried

to this place, twigs & pebbles; then the boat, Inner Farne, a dead rabbit discovered at Cuthbert's font. The second; the Valley of Desolation was first, Maiden Castle was third.

Where else; Manorbier, Peak District, gritstone, Dorset chalk dome, Glastonbury – his meanings. Pulling himself into thread & taking the whole horror in his dreams. He aims at tokens of the light: Year of the Rabbit. The fear of/the hope for children. Christian shrines therefore. And pagan hill sites. Confusion.

The local Lud-town calculations emerge out of body-block, low weather – can't handle the increasing speed. Receives Doug Oliver's *In The Cave of Suicession*. This is a large clue & description of what-is-going-on, unseen. The lust of the land. Dressed imperatives chisel their questions into rock. Also rips through, in a single sitting, Winthrop Palmer Boswell's *Irish Wizards in the Woods of Ethiopia* & *The Snake in the Grove*: crackpot, money-fed, post-thesoid truths. Another piece of the times to swallow. We are gathered again, intersection, return, barbarous friendships share the hospice, aim at the temple. So much has been cut away. We jitter & shake with a new confidence.

They have circumnavigated the Roman Wall, they have followed the Hawksmoor trail east, from Blake's grave & the glimpse of St Luke's, Old Street, through the Rookeries & refuse laneways & streets of bird fear, the fen edge, to the place of the lichen-pattern on the grave, to the crossroads, the staked vampire pit, St-George's-in-the-East; Limehouse, twilight, locked into the church, the girl is bearing a child, first weeks of life, & is exhausted from the walk, & falls asleep here, in the darkness, & dreams, while we stand at the foot of the wooden staircase – & she cannot, reasonably, face the continued journey down the length of the Isle of Dogs – hesitation at the Anubic border point – swirl of london transport – hop a bus to the tunnel-head – under the river – Greenwich – Alfege – Hawksmoor's first & our final point – the hill the observatory the old palace – after the muds & savagery we climb – Maze Hill the light – pulsing dome of stars – we would wish ourselves transformed – we would pursue this optimism to the last feet of the Island – & with all the ferocity of a boar hunt.

His companions visit the Steiner farm; are about, this day, to depart for America, Lindisfarne Community, a study group on the Book of Revelations – as I am about to depart for Wales, Manorbier, birthplace of Giraldus Cambrensis, land held by Bledri ap Cadivor, Jesse Weston's candidate for Grail authorship – late afternoon, suitcases, night drive ahead – & it comes on him to act out the oracle run – the idea had been there a long time (two days, a week, six months?) – the shrine uncovered by instinct & by calculation.

It has been told how the Hawksmoor churches yield the symbol of Set, the tool for castration & the instrument for impressing cuneiform script onto the clay table – he now calculates the central point of the horizontal bar of the T – the point of force, of maximum push. This is drawn out on the map, crudely at first, on a London A to Z, & then, more accurately, on the Master Map of Greater London. The point given is an epicentre of energies – & known to us already – from the walks preparatory to filming *Maggot Street* – the journey made in nervous optimism & openair hope – returning to find the garden dug up, the hall, the floorboards, the bedroom – massive gas-leak & potential holocaust.

The point is sited on the Northern Sewage Outflow, raised Ridgeway, slanting south-east, Crows Road, East London Cemetery, Saxon Road, running into the Thames at Barking Creek. But the shrine is at the precise spot where this secret route passes above the River Lea – the ancient English/Danish border, as ratified by the Treaty of Wedmore (878). The oracle-mark is also an extension of the arrow – where Old Ford Road blends with Roman Road. That crossing place. The hurdle-ford of the east. The invasion path, the path of escape. From this platform we look down on Iceland Street & Autumn Street, we look across water & waste & nomansland to Stratford (Chobham Farm workday industrial memories) – the route of Los again ("thro' Hackney ... towards London / Till he came to old Stratford, & thence to Stepney & the Isle / of Leutha's Dogs, thence thro' the narrows of the River's side").

He knew that it had to be RUN. This was a thing for total body exhaustion – "annihilated in the old retort of an unflinching will". He knew the route, in intimate absent-minded loss, & NEEDED the word – but as he ran he understood ("when revelation comes athlete & sage are merged") that all he would get this time was the sound of blood pumping in the throat, harsh lung – which he could interpret as oracular confirmation that this was the route.

It is raining, without intensity. He turns out of Albion Drive into Queensbridge Road, south, over Suicide Bridge, where the Krays offered their weapons to the water after the mutilation & death of Jack the Hat. He follows the thick green serpent jelly of the canal. Rain falls like lead shot, denting the surface; rings of opening & closing eyes. High flood level, the rush. Uneven cobble ground, back of the flats, garages. No strain as he runs, the idea is motor. A flame across his chest. Lung-Gom, is the aim.

Sir Walter Scott (re-built 1909) to his left; the urinal, to his right. Sheep Lane, old slaughter track to London Fields, the drover's pen. Ash Grove. And across the major traffic-ditch of Mare Street. Gore Road bends into Victoria Park by the north-west gate.

Here he is tourist to the circuit of Reg Kray's early morning constitutionals. There is the renewed energy of high elm avenues & the canal is his immediate companion once more. They are ringing the closing bell. Darkness covers his ritual. False light. Shapes in the dusk shift & muffle the rhythm of his feet, his forced breath.

He passes the plaster dog guardian effigies, the Anubic warnings, twins. The lake is on his left, depth, muddy density, the concentration screen for the dipping consciousness of a line of gathered invalid carriages, convalescent motor cars, adulteries, first outings of the new born.

Out of the gate, holds for the traffic, the light stream, his eye open for Arthur's car, Grove Road. And on into the eastern segment of the park, the hunting grounds, the people's woodland. They are chaining the gates behind him. His chest prepares a question, over grass, over root bumps, wave-patterns in the soft ground; slight climb to Gunmaker's Lane.

He is entering the corridor of mysteries. It is out of his control. The wind in the tree grove. The canal is now dry. It has been drained. Banks of mud. And the smell of it. Objects in the mud. The rain hammering down.

He turns away from the park, climbs over the gate, twin globes mounted on pyramid plinths, out into Parnell Road. A tin horse outside the corner shop. They are returning to the flats. Gas ignition of tea hour. Colour fuse of television in high windows. Multiple repeated image & word. Connecting with the serpent. Wick Lane. Dips into a road tunnel. Bone echo, footfall. Concrete slabs, sarsen conglomerate. Climb above the abandoned building, the place of injections. And onto the raised way, the sewage outflow path – the grid of city lights – industrial flare – Percy Dalton's Peanuts – the Safety Tread – bursts towards the marked place – the ritual site – the last yards at full sprint – to empty the body of all resistance – to fall upon the ground – swollen ear pressed to the wet grass.

The building is a war relic, meaningless & abandoned. Grey machine-gun bunker with four related step-obstacles set across the track to the south. It is hidden in a thatch of weed & thorn. It is directly above the waters. Lea river to north & south. He listens. He drags his cheek against the pebble-dash. He wants the blood word. He circumnavigates the building, anti-clockwise, pushing through the wire growth. It is a six-sided enclosure; relating to so many other high-energy structures – the original Spitle Field, his dream, the old map of the city,

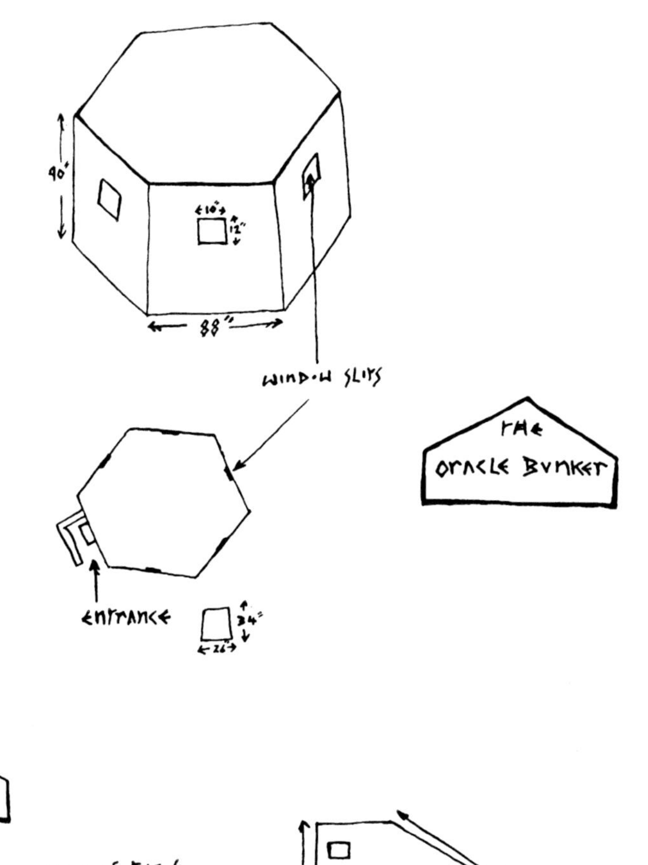
90"
10"
12"
88"
WINDOW SLITS
THE
ORACLE BUNKER
ENTRANCE
34"
26"

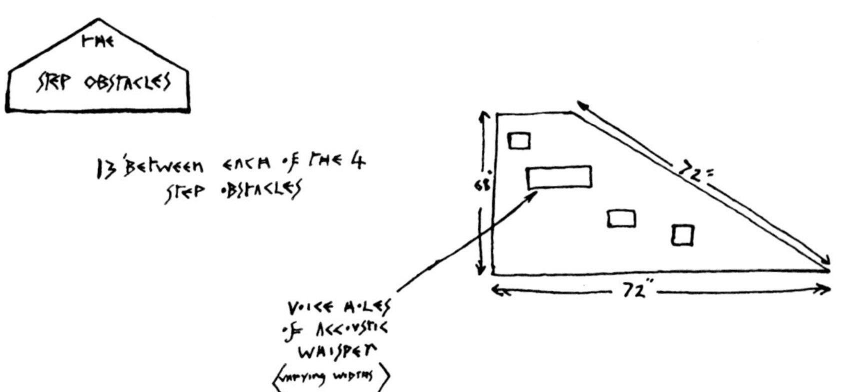
THE
STEP OBSTACLES
13' BETWEEN EACH OF THE 4
STEP OBSTACLES
68"
72"
72"
VOICE HOLES
OF ACCOUSTIC
WHISPER
(VARYING WIDTHS)

hexagonal field on the hill rim – the fence that traps the Cerne Abbas Hercules giant – the sheep-pen that Turner locates in his sketch of Llanthony Abbey – the stock-exchange booths. Feels for it, understands that it has meaning: does not know what that meaning is.

All this is darkness. He crawls, in the machine throb & thump & heavy chemical night, into the entrance of the bunker. Pillar supports. A chair. Urinal smell. Rat fears. Small window slits. No word; no word is, or could be, given. No word other than – a black workman passes along the outflow, north – no word other than the need for it. He is relieved of the tension of the block of the desire to run. Is eager to get out into the air, to turn for home. Pauses a moment. After rain, clear sky. The star dome is sharp above him. He knows nothing of the precisions & mechanics & movements & meanings here either. An ignorant man, ground-held, muddy in motive – he jogs back the way he came.

24/7/75: browsing in Tower Hamlets Library, late afternoon, low energy weathers & discover item confirming heat of instinct in siting Oracle Shrine. A coffin, 7' wide, excavated at Old Ford, 1867, "of one piece of stone, the inside having been hewn & chipped out", origin & age unknown, removed from the earth "close to the old Roman Road, which was the high road from Middlesex into Essex, over the ford of the River Lea." So again we service the dead, complete the stifled gesture, grasp at the arm raised in salute from the choked ground.

Afterword

No mere pasquinader, Iain Sinclair, larking, drags from London's amniotic silt the trove of centuries and presents it to us, still dripping, still stinking, still caked and frequently still defiantly kicking. In a series of ever more ambitious raree shows, ring-mastered with a mixture of relish and horror, with sly Celtic magic, with almost supernatural control, he has established himself as London's most original celebrant and one of her great creative voices. Peter Ackroyd, another subtle London visionary who has much in common with Sinclair, enthusiastically points to *Lud Heat* as an inspirer of his time-travelling *Hawksmoor*. Sinclair always leads my own imagination back to its true territory.

At its best London fiction has, in the past twenty years, become characteristically a visionary medium. In contrast to the rational, neatly written disappointments of Old Sir Kingsley, we have a Gilrayish Young Martin, as unEnlightened as they come, sifting the Sunday morning Portobello gutters for revelations and gagging like Swift. We have the unfortunate Rushdie, not quite suffering almost the noblest fate of any visionary, and Fay Weldon and, these days, even A. S. Byatt. To those of us who have been exploring the territory for some time, it looked like everyone started knocking back the laudanum and investigating the paranormal pretty much as soon as a handy tourist trail had been blazed to the high ground where angels live. Territory penetrated and mapped long-since by Sinclair and other extra-mural romantics like Angela Carter; Philip K. Dick and J. G. Ballard in largely unpublicised expeditions since the mid-1960s.

It could be argued that the Occult has in the nick of time come to the aid of a threatened Orthodoxy. Talismans and omens are eagerly snapped up by a technologically challenged middle class. Some days, any old bone will do. Little visionary peels are slipped into Professor Lodge's jellies. The modern English novel contains almost as many ghosts and visitations as a Radcliffe three-decker. Spontaneous combustion should soon become an acceptable literary convention. A larger measure of supernatural melodrama is allowed to English domestic fiction than at any time since *Northanger Abbey* put a welcome lid on the Gothic's groaning trick coffin. Fifty-year-old notions of pulp SF writers become novel and exciting elements to spice the traditional mix. No wonder all these people are obsessed with vampires and rejuvenation formulae.

Most of the recycling undertaken by English fiction's best known careerists is about as effective as a Hampstead green bin in evading the inevitability of decay and death or even disguising that familiar, rather unpleasant sweetish smell. A bit of genre-borrowing isn't really the same thing as owning an original vision, but at least those grave-robbers and wine-waterers, those croppers and colons, helped produce the climactic shift which now allows a writer as original as Iain Sinclair to find the larger audience he has deserved for years.

He started showing up in high-street bookshops with a tangle of bombsite brambles and gaudy fireweed, the contents of long-buried basements, the muttering bones and whispering rags of his book-dealer's trawls through a city largely unexplored by her own inhabitants and thus insufficiently respected or feared, which he called *White Chappell, Scarlet Tracings*. He followed this with a structurally more sophisticated *Downriver* and then gave his widening readership *Radon Daughters* as glorious proof of his ever-increasing powers. A manipulative Harlequin slipping through the alleys and twitterns between one world and another, one supernatural realm and another, one age and another, weaving what at close perspective sometimes seems a chaotic course. Sinclair is an authentic visionary. Only at the end of a book, however, do we realise we've also been in the power of a genuine wizard, someone capable of tracing patterns and designs only barely perceptible to most people and, more to the point, able to reveal them to us.

Iain Sinclair's rich enthusiasms, his relish for the idiosyncratic, the original and profoundly grotesque gives his work a certain Dickensian flavour – but Sinclair's never as desperate as Dickens to discover hope. His literary heroes are Hodgson, Burroughs, the beats, the best pulp writers – all people madly in love with their own powers of language, their own massive turbulences, their own impossible paradoxes, their own perceptions of non-linear Time, of coexistent past, present and future, forever seeking to communicate the ecstasy of their unguarded souls to an average reader who has come to look to books for consolation, not inspiration.

Sinclair works as a revenant, a publicist, an archivist of the marginal, the unfashionable and the self-doomed, against the general tenor of Eng. lit. power politics whose vested interests permit no real assault on the status quo, where the established canon is forcefully promoted because lazy convention also acts to employ academics, critics and literary editors at good wages for small effort. The old catholics like Walter Raleigh or Quiller-Couch, who founded our English schools, were soon replaced in the early 20th century by ambitious puritans, low Tories or worse.

It's against a tide hazardous with rotting driftwood, snapping predators and the not-quite-dead, queer lights reflecting from his benign dome, his terrifying glasses, that Sinclair poles his stately punt. He has a book-dealer's eye for obscurity and rarity, a way of spotting something which, until he fishes it out and polishes it up a bit, we hadn't ourselves noticed among the ordinary, the disgusting or even alarming flotsam of London's endless flux. Sinclair's people are no more bizarre or grotesque than most real people. That is to say, they are often, like Dickens's, larger than fiction, but in no way larger than life.

Sinclair celebrates what is idiosyncratic in men and women, yet no character is stranger or more quirkily obsessed than half the people you'd meet on a long train trip. You always leave Sinclair, as you leave Rembrandt or Hals, looking at the familiar world with freshly informed eyes.

Sinclair's relish for language, for lost words and forgotten notions, his lust for metaphor, links him with earlier London visionaries like Blake or Eliot, just as the breadth of his enthusiasms allows the inspiration of Ginsberg and De Quincey, but it's neither his eclecticism nor his influences which define his work – it's his curiosity, his sense of justice, his bardic instincts, his generosity, and above all his original vision of what remains in spite of everything the greatest and most complex of all cities. He proves to us why London is still the best and most rewarding place for a poet or a novelist to live.

He proves it through celebrations like this.

Michael Moorcock
Lost Pines, Texas
April 1995

Lightning Source UK Ltd.
Milton Keynes UK
UKOW050207300113

205585UK00002B/332/P

9 781908 011602